PUI ... ORS

# INTO the SPOTLIGHT

Carrie Hope Fletcher is an actress, singer and vlogger. Carrie has starred in a number of shows on London's West End and on national theatre tours. She has written several books for adults and has had numerous number one bestsellers.

Carrie's first book for children, *Into the Spotlight*, is inspired by Noel Streatfeild's beloved novel, *Ballet Shoes*, and has been endorsed by the Streatfeild estate.

Carrie lives just outside London with her boyfriend, Oliver, her tuxedo cat, Edgar, and numerous fictional friends that she keeps on bookshelves, just in case.

**Follow Carrie on Twitter**
**@CarrieHFletcher**

# INTO the SPOTLIGHT

# CARRIE HOPE FLETCHER

Illustrated by *Kiersten Eagan*

PUFFIN

PUFFIN BOOKS

UK | USA | Canada | Ireland | Australia
India | New Zealand | South Africa

Puffin Books is part of the Penguin Random House group of companies
whose addresses can be found at global.penguinrandomhouse.com.

www.penguin.co.uk
www.puffin.co.uk
www.ladybird.co.uk

Penguin
Random House
UK

First published 2020
This paperback edition published 2021

001

Text copyright © Carrie Hope Fletcher, 2020
Illustrations copyright © Kiersten Eagan, 2020

The moral right of the author and illustrator has been asserted

Typeset by Jouve (UK), Milton Keynes
Printed and bound in Great Britain by Clays Ltd, Elcograf S.p.A.

A CIP catalogue record for this book is available from the British Library

The authorized representative in the EEA is Penguin Random House Ireland,
Morrison Chambers, 32 Nassau Street, Dublin D02 YH68

ISBN: 978–0–241–46211–9

All correspondence to:
Puffin Books
Penguin Random House Children's
One Embassy Gardens, 8 Viaduct Gardens, London SW11 7BW

*To every child who reads this book, dream your dreams as BIG as you can because sometimes we grow into them.*

# Contents

1. Lost and Found     1

2. A Name for Ourselves     9

3. The Pebble Family     13

4. Boys Don't Dance     23

5. In Mabel We Believe     32

6. The Voice Inside Marigold's Head     38

7. A Blast from the Past     47

8. The History Books     59

9. The Jig Is Up     75

10. Bam Returns     79

11. Listening at the Door     82

12. Petrova     93

13. The Woman in Pink     99

| | | |
|---|---|---|
| 14. | Hope for Breakfast | 106 |
| 15. | Morris's Idea | 113 |
| 16. | No Room for Worry | 122 |
| 17. | A New Show in Town | 131 |
| 18. | A Visit to Wonderland | 138 |
| 19. | A Colourful Personality | 146 |
| 20. | Mack Needs Help | 155 |
| 21. | The Empty Shelves | 168 |
| 22. | Rain, Rain, Go Away! | 176 |
| 23. | The Power of the Internet | 192 |
| 24. | Opening Night | 206 |
| 25. | Plunged into Darkness | 216 |
| 26. | Trixabellina von Hustle the Third | 228 |
| 27. | A Happy Ending | 235 |
| | Acknowledgements | 245 |

# 1

# Lost and Found

The Pebble children lived underneath Chelsea Bridge. Well, they lived underneath the railway arches next to Chelsea Bridge, which is closer to Pimlico, but it felt fancier for them to say they lived in Chelsea. It was much too far to walk to the Natural History Museum to see the dinosaurs, but close enough to Battersea Park Children's Zoo for them not to complain too much. Not that they often complained. The Pebbles were very contented children. After all, what children wouldn't be content when living in a theatre? A theatre was a wonderful place to live. It was filled with the most interesting people. Especially Pebble Theatre. It was called this because from wall to wall, top to bottom, it was covered in pebbles collected from seasides all over the world by someone they called B.A.M.

'Bam told me this one is her favourite, because when you tilt your head and squint a bit it looks like Elvis Presley,' said Marigold, the eldest Pebble child. All three children tilted their heads and squinted but only Marigold really knew what Elvis Presley had looked like. Bam, by the way, is the fastest way the children had found to say 'Brilliant Aunt Maude'.

'Great-aunt Maude?' Bam had scoffed when called 'Great-aunt Maude' by her great-niece, Lydia. 'I'm better than *great*. I'm *BRRRILLIANT*!' she trilled as she flourished her long, pointed bright-red nails round her short, curled silver hair. Bam owned Pebble Theatre and she travelled the earth looking for the world's finest talent to bring back to perform on its stage. She'd found contortionists, opera singers, playwrights and magicians. The weirder the talent, the more excited Bam got. However, she never went anywhere without finding a seaside town or a beach and searching for a pebble to bring home and add to her collection. There were pale pink ones that were pointed and jagged and looked like the teeth of a ferocious sea creature. There was a shiny green one that Morris could stare at for hours, hypnotized by the way it sometimes turned orange if the light hit it just right. There were ones so blue they looked like little pieces of the ocean. Bam brought them home and stuck them to the walls of the theatre. There were pebbles of all colours, shapes and sizes absolutely everywhere. They were even on the ceiling! Bam had created a wondrous seaside cavern. However, her favourite additions to her collection were the young Marigold, Mabel and Morris.

Twelve years ago, Bam found herself on Varkala Beach in India, looking out at the ocean, feeling peaceful and at ease with herself despite the hot sun beating down upon her shoulders. Her already wrinkled skin was beginning to crackle and peel but Bam was just pleased to be out of the cold English rain. Suddenly, a violent wave crashed on to the shore, shaking Bam out of her calm daze. A basket gently rolled out of the water and washed up at her feet. Just before the tide pulled it back into the ocean, Bam took hold of the basket's handle and lifted it away.

However, the weight of it took her by surprise. At first, Bam thought it was only filled with pretty orange flowers but, as the sound of the crashing waves died down, she could now hear the sound of a soft wailing. Bam crouched in the wet sand, careful not to let her dress touch the water, and there, in among the marigolds, was the beautiful face of a baby. Her eyes were golden like the flowers that surrounded her and, without thinking, Bam lifted the child to her chest and cradled her until she hushed its cries.

She tried hard to locate the child's parents but eventually found that they had drowned when their boat went down at sea, and that she had no remaining family. Brilliant Aunt Maude took the child to the Indian adoption authorities, but, when she tried to hand the baby over, the little creature clung on to Bam's shirt and started bawling. Bam knew in that moment that she wasn't able to leave the darling girl behind and so officially adopted her, but without telling her great-niece. When she arrived home with more than just luggage, Lydia was less than calm.

'A baby?!' Lydia cried as Brilliant Aunt Maude crashed through the stage door of the theatre, dragging her case with one arm and cradling a baby in the other. Lydia took the child from her, her mouth flapping open and closed, unable to believe she was actually holding an infant in her arms. Lydia had always dreamt of having a child one day but her hectic job had kept her awfully busy and led her down a different path. Now in her mid-thirties, she hadn't dared to hope of raising a little one for a long time but the moment she caught sight of this sleeping cherub, her heart swelled and very almost burst with joy.

'Yes, I'm quite certain that's what it is,' said Bam as she removed her coat, happy to be home.

'Of course I know it's a baby, but *whose* baby is it? And what's it doing here?' The baby began to wake in her arms and, like a natural, Lydia began to coo and rock her back and forth.

'Well, I thought *you* could look after her. I've named her Marigold, after the flowers she was lying in when I found her.' And that was the end of the conversation. Lydia knew there was little else that could be said to persuade Brilliant Aunt Maude otherwise. Marigold was now part of the family.

Next came Mabel. When Marigold was two, Bam had been called away to Portobello Beach in Scotland. Her younger cousin Bartholomew lived there, and he was not well. In fact, he was not very well at all. After Bartholomew's wife passed away, Bam was the only family he had left and Bam had managed to get to his bedside just in time for Bartholomew to place his baby daughter in her care before he closed his eyes for the last time. His passing was only eased by the little girl he left behind. A little girl who looked so much like her father that Bam felt a lump in her throat every time she looked into her eyes.

Bam wiped tears from her cheeks as she carefully passed the bundle to Lydia.

'You did the right thing,' Lydia said, but as she looked down at the sleeping child she caught sight of a flash of red underneath the blanket. She uncovered the baby's head and the brightest red curls pinged out in one great burst. The little girl wriggled, then opened her eyes to reveal they were a deep green. Lydia was lost immediately.

'Does she have a name?'

'Mabel. Named after a character in my cousin's favourite musical.'

'As in *Mack and Mabel*?'

'Exactly.' Bam smiled. And that was the end of the conversation. Lydia knew there was little else to be said. Mabel was now part of the family.

Last but not least, Morris appeared. He was the only child who found Bam before Bam had a chance to find him. One cold November morning, when the sun had barely risen, Bam made her way from their home above the theatre through the corridors, past dressing rooms, past the stage, through the foyer and out in front of the building. She often liked to do this. When no one was around, she would nip outside to look up at the theatre that she'd worked so hard for. She would stand with her hands on her hips and revel in the pride that rose all the way up from her tummy to where it would shine out of her face in a smile — a smile that was almost as bright as the sign that told the world that this was the Pebble Theatre. On this particular day, however, before she opened the door to the theatre, she noticed there was a red shoebox sitting on the steps with FRAGILE: HANDLE WITH CARE written across the side in bold lettering.

Hurriedly she turned the key in the lock and skittered out in her slippers, pulling her dressing gown round her. Her breath puffed out of her mouth in the chilly air. As she bent over the shoebox, she saw that it did not contain the pair of trainers it might once have done, but instead a tiny, wriggling human! The poor thing was freezing to the touch. Bam quickly scooped up the baby, shoebox and all, and ran back inside, screaming for Lydia.

'What's all the fuss? What is it?' Lydia ran out of her bedroom and into the kitchen, rubbing her eyes. Here, Bam had settled the shoebox on the table and was now holding the baby as close to her as possible, willing her own warmth into its tiny body.

'It's a little boy!' Bam said, out of breath from the commotion.

'Not again.' Lydia sighed, feeling as though she was stuck in a time warp.

'Now, you can't pin the blame on me, Lydia. *This* one found *me*.'

'Where did he come from, I wonder?' Lydia asked. But, as she picked up the shoebox, a small letter fluttered out from between its folded cardboard edges.

'Oh!' Lydia read it aloud.

### Please take great care of him.

'How could this happen?' A sob caught in Lydia's throat.

'The world makes people desperate,' Bam said gently, shaking her head. 'Not to worry. He's one of *us* now. Was there a name? In the letter?' Lydia turned the paper over in her hands to make certain, but it was just the one simple line scrawled across the page.

'No, I'm afraid not.'

'Then it's down to me again! How about . . .' The cogs in Bam's head began to turn. Lydia peered into the bundle. His skin was dark and now warming up under Bam's embrace and his cheeks were so round Lydia had a sudden urge to squeeze them between her fingers. Before Bam could think of a suitable name, Lydia made a suggestion of her own. A name that belonged to her great-uncle, Bam's late husband. A man who had the warmest hugs, the kindest eyes and always saw the best in people.

'How about Morris?' Lydia said.

Bam looked from Lydia to the wispy-haired cherub in her arms and back to Lydia. Bam's breath caught but she quickly swallowed down the lump of feelings that had formed in her throat.

'Marigold, Mabel and Morris.' Bam grinned. And that was the end of the conversation. Morris was now part of the family and he was the last child to find his way to the Pebble Theatre.

# 2

# A Name for Ourselves

Lydia worked at the Pebble Theatre as the stage manager. A stage manager is someone awfully clever who is in charge of just about everything that goes on backstage! She was responsible for lots of things, including organizing rehearsals, and arranging costume and wig fittings for all of the actors. Then, when the show was finally up and running, Lydia *kept* it running. She made sure everyone had their props on time, cued entrances and exits, and even made everyone tea in the interval. On top of all of *that*, she also looked after the three children when Bam was on her travels – which was more often than not.

'Lydia,' said three-year-old Morris, as he curled up on Bam's niece's lap. It was bedtime and Lydia had just read them a story, but the three children were not tired and knew that the best way to stay up late was to ask Lydia lots of questions that needed very long, complicated answers. 'Lydia, do you think Bam has forgotten us?' Morris pouted.

'I should hope not! That would mean she's also forgotten about me, and I'm far too amazing to be forgotten, aren't I?' Lydia tickled Morris until he told her just how amazing she was. Lydia had dark chocolate-coloured hair that blended in with the black headset she had to wear when she was backstage. It had one big earphone that covered her right ear and a little microphone that curled round her cheek so that she could talk to people all over the theatre. The children saw her so often with her headset on that she looked strange at bedtime when she wasn't wearing it, rather like when you're so used to seeing someone wearing glasses that they almost look like a totally different person when they take them off at the end of the day. Lydia always took the headset off before entering the children's room, so her head wasn't filled with other people's voices and she could give them her full attention.

'Lydia?' Mabel, who was now five, asked as she rested her little head on Lydia's knee. Mabel's burnt-orange hair spilt over her face and Lydia smiled as she began to plait it, ready for bed. It was almost as long as Mabel was tall and Lydia was always a little worried that she might get tangled up in it in the night. 'What's our last name?' Now this was a much more serious question, because Lydia didn't have an answer.

'Hmm,' she said, concentrating on plaiting. 'Well, let's see. You can have *my* last name if you like. It's Crawley.'

'Like a creepy-crawly?' said Morris, scrunching up his nose. Mabel reached across to him and gave his arm a nudge.

'Sorry.' Morris buried his head in Lydia's shoulder.

'Exactly like a creepy-crawly.' She smiled. 'OK, not Crawley. How about Cooper? That's Bam's last name. How about that?' Morris and Mabel looked at each other and then at Marigold, who was sitting on her bed reading her own book. Marigold was seven and the two younger siblings felt it was her responsibility to deny taking Cooper as their last name. Being the eldest made Marigold the most responsible and the other two looked up to her. She had wise eyes and a quiet nature, which made Mabel and Morris both a little nervous.

'Cooper sounds a little bit . . . well . . . boring,' said Marigold.

'Don't let Bam hear you say that!' Lydia snorted.

'It's a good name,' Marigold remedied. 'It just doesn't feel like it really belongs to *us*.' Mabel and Morris nodded their agreement. Marigold closed her book and thought for a moment.

'What about . . . Pebble?' Marigold said. Morris and Mabel grinned at each other and then back at Marigold.

11

'Pebble?' Lydia raised an eyebrow. 'After the theatre?'

'Exactly. No one else will have a name like it. It'll be all our own.' Morris and Mabel nodded enthusiastically but looked wide-eyed to Lydia, whose face burst into a grin.

'I think that's a marvellous idea. After all, you are Bam's favourite additions to her collection. It only seems right that you all be Pebbles.'

The children all jumped to their feet and shouted, 'HOORAY!'

'How do you do? I'm Marigold *Pebble*,' said Marigold holding out her hand, which Lydia shook. She danced out of the way and the others followed suit.

'How do you do? I'm Mabel *Pebble*.' Mabel almost couldn't speak for laughter.

'HOW DO YOU DO!' Morris bellowed. 'I'M MORRIS PEBBLE AND MY SISTERS AND I HAVE THE BEST NAME ON PLANET EARTH!' The newly appointed Pebbles collapsed into a giggling heap on the floor, happiness pouring out of them, feeling a little more complete than they did before.

# 3

# The Pebble Family

The Pebble Theatre was home to many an interesting person. It was partly why the Pebble children couldn't imagine spending their summer anywhere else. Every summer Lydia asked if maybe they would like to go on holiday to the seaside, but with all the pebbles it already felt so much like a seaside that it seemed pointless.

'What about a summer camp?' Lydia had once suggested, but the children became so sad at the notion of being sent away that Lydia never mentioned it again. The children loved the theatre, and the occupants of the theatre loved them. So it was settled that the children would always spend their summer helping Lydia backstage. As they grew older their responsibilities became bigger and more important, which meant every year the children were even more excited.

Always, on the first day of the summer holidays, the Pebble children would go from dressing room to dressing room to say an official 'hello' to everyone. The Pebble Theatre seemed to be like a warm bed in the middle of winter – somewhere people didn't want to leave. Whenever someone new arrived, they found a way to be part of every show whether there was a role for them on stage or not, and so a strange little family had formed. It had been a long time since Bam had found any new performers for the theatre, but its current company were loyal and hard-working.

Although their theatrical family was small, the Pebble children counted down the seconds to their summer holiday when they were allowed to help out backstage and join in the fun. Bam was the head of their happy family and her trips away had become shorter and shorter ever since the children had come into her life – but this year, this particular adventure of hers seemed to be taking quite some time. Whenever Bam was away there were plenty of other people in the theatre to keep the children entertained. Cora, the theatre's stage prompt, was particularly good fun. Cora sat by the side of the stage at the prompt desk. Morris often liked to think of Cora as the puppetmaster of the show because it was her job to make sure all the lights, sound effects and pieces of set all worked and moved at the right time. He would often sneak downstairs after bedtime and sit behind Cora, watching her delicately turn the script's pages, press glowing orange buttons and whisper into her headset. She created a kind of magic that no one in the audience could see – but no one was more grateful for Cora than her husband, Layton. He was an older actor, whose memory was like that of a goldfish. Part of Cora's job was to read out lines from the script should an actor ever forget them, which Layton very often did.

Morris always teased Marigold for idolizing Dawson Sanders. He was in his mid-forties but still looked like a dashing leading man, and he always wore a suit, trench coat and trilby when he wasn't on stage. Dawson was rather serious, but it was only because he was awfully nervous and got dreadful stage fright. He liked to be left alone before a show so he could run all of his lines over and over. However, because he was so stern and rarely ever said a word, most of the time the children left him alone. Dawson's husband, on the other hand, was the life and soul of the theatre on account of his excellent magic tricks. In particular, Dante was very good at sleight of hand with his pack of cards. Mabel was especially mesmerized, and, just when she thought she had figured out the workings of one trick, he astounded her with yet another. She found it frustrating and impressive in equal measure.

Kitty and Claudia were probably the most eccentric of the

theatre's company due to the fact that they never wore anything other than matching tights and leotards, often in very bright colours. At seventy-two years of age, Kitty and Claudia were a dancing duo like no other. Their speciality was tap dancing and sometimes their shoes moved so fast you weren't sure whose feet were whose! Although the tapping twin sisters adored each other, their bickering and squabbling could be heard up and down the corridors of the theatre. The children found them entertaining to watch when they worked together and pulled off incredible dance routines, but found them a little scary when they started to row!

Theodore Rosenbaum was the resident stuntman. Bam had found him on a movie set in the centre of London looking glum as he waited for the next scene. He said he was tired of travelling and wished he could find one spot to settle in, where he could live and work and feel like part of a family again. Bam couldn't believe her luck. Pebble Theatre was the perfect place for him. He could teach stage combat and make stunts look real, and yet make sure everyone was safe and unharmed. But when Bam brought him home to the theatre, she hadn't prepared the children for his arrival. While Theodore was the gentlest man you could ever hope to meet, with perfect manners and a heart of gold, he was also six foot seven and as wide as all three children standing together shoulder to shoulder – and he was tattooed from the top of his head right down to his littlest toe! Poor Morris was only two when Theodore first arrived and got quite a fright, having never seen anyone as tall or tattooed before – although it wasn't long before Morris realized that Theodore's height meant that he gave the best piggybacks.

And finally there was Mack, the ginger theatre cat brought in to chase away the mice but often found chasing after Mabel. The day Bam brought him home, he escaped out of the children's room and got lost inside the theatre. No one knew how long he must have been mewing before Mabel found him above the stage, stuck in the rafters. She rescued him and brought him down to safety, so Bam rewarded her with being the one to name him. Mabel decided to name him Mack, to complete the name of her father's favourite musical, *Mack and Mabel*. Ever since then, Mack had rarely strayed far from Mabel's side. Marigold and Morris were exceptionally jealous that he gave her the most attention. They tried their hardest to get his interest, but he'd only come if he heard the sound of Mabel's voice calling him. He would sleep at the bottom of her bed if she was feeling a little sad and her lap was the only one he would sit on – even though it drove her mad that her clothes were always covered in his ginger fur.

Mack was often found near the stage door next to a little portable heater that was meant for Petunia, the woman who worked there. If you were part of the theatre family, she was the first person you'd see when you entered and the last person you'd see when you left. The children called her 'The

Keeper of the Keys'. This was because behind her desk was a little wooden box mounted on the wall that contained every key for every door in the theatre. Each key was golden, but they were all different shapes and sizes. Some were very small indeed but unlocked giant doors that took all three children to push open. Some were plain while others were twisted into ornate shapes, but each key was as intriguing as the last. At some point in their childhood, each Pebble had become fascinated with the box of keys but Petunia was very strict.

'Now, you see, children, each key is unique and opens just one door. No two keys are the same and so, if one is lost, we can never open that door again.' Petunia let them look at the box but they were never to touch and it was locked every night with a special key of its own that Petunia wore on a piece of string round her neck. Aside from being keeper of the keys, Petunia was an excellent storyteller and was very good at telling the children stories about themselves. She'd make them hold out their palms and, just by looking at the lines and wrinkles on their hands, she would be able to tell the most peculiar details. Like how long they were going to live for, if they were passionate and adventurous, and whether fate was going to intervene in their lives one day.

The Pebble Theatre's play for this summer was *The Dumb Waiter* by Harold Pinter. It was the same play they had done for the last three summers, because it only required two actors and currently the theatre only had two actors at its disposal.

'This play is so *boooooring*,' complained Mabel.

'I know.' Morris yawned. 'Why doesn't Bam just hire more actors?' Morris was picking the cracked paint off one of the walls backstage, as they watched the show from the wings.

'It costs a lot of money to hire actors and if Bam can't even give this place a lick of paint,' Marigold said, slapping Morris's hands back from the giant hole he'd peeled away, 'I doubt she can afford to hire more people than she needs to.'

'Will you stop picking at the paint, Morris!' Lydia suddenly appeared from the darkness of the wings. 'There'll be nothing left by the time you've finished!'

'Sorry, Lydia,' Morris moaned.

'I've already had to fix the door handle on Layton's dressing room. He was stuck in there for a whole hour before Theodore heard him calling for help. The drains have backed up again so it's all a bit whiffy backstage and I've got to call someone about that . . .' Lydia was still rattling off her to-do list as she skittered away, collecting props from shelves and piling them up high in her arms.

'Does Lydia seem a little more . . . tense than usual?' Marigold asked. Morris shrugged.

'Maybe a little. She's always like this at the start of a show, though,' Mabel said.

'Hmmm,' Marigold replied, unconvinced.

'I'm sure she's fine, Marigold.' Mabel smiled, shaking her sister's shoulder playfully as if she were trying to shake the worry out of her. 'It's Lydia! When is she not tense?'

'Oh, no.' Marigold put her hand on Mabel's shoulder and squeezed. It was only then that Mabel and Morris noticed just how quiet it was. 'Layton's forgotten his lines again.' Layton had paused for so long that the audience, as little as it was, had started to murmur among themselves quite noticeably. The children ran down the wing, through something called a 'crossover', which is a corridor hidden at the back of the stage that links stage left and stage right, and into the wing where Cora was sitting.

'I said . . . I've brought a few biscuits,' Dawson repeated his line more slowly.

'Well . . . well . . .'

'You'd better eat them quick then!' Cora whispered furiously from the wing.

'Pardon?' Layton whispered back.

'The silly old fool's forgotten to put his hearing aid on. I'm surprised he's got this far.' Cora put her head in her hands.

'Well, you'd better eat them quick then!' the children hissed together.

'Well, the feta cheese is thick, Ben,' Layton said. The audience guffawed and Layton went bright red in the face. Dawson carried on as best he could over the laughter. Mabel disappeared for a few seconds through a door that led to the auditorium. 'People are leaving,' she said sadly upon her return.

'Nothing to be done except carry on. The show must go on!' Cora said, lifting her head out of her sweaty palms, turning back to the script and readjusting her headset. It was then that Dawson's spotlight turned off with a giant clunk. Some of the audience gasped and then grumbled but Dawson, with the same resilience as Cora, continued saying his lines.

'There won't be any audience left by the interval!' said Marigold.

'Even if there's one person in that audience, they'll carry on. I doubt Layton and Dawson will stop for anything,' Cora explained, following the lines in her script with a finger. The Pebble children exchanged a concerned look and quietly retreated back along the wing and up to their bedroom.

'Was the theatre in this much trouble last summer?' Mabel asked.

'What do you mean?' Morris frowned.

'Everything just seems like it's . . . falling apart,' Mabel replied.

'Oh, don't be so silly. Layton only forgot a few lines and the electrics in this place have always been a bit iffy. You're being dramatic.' Morris rolled his eyes and skipped ahead up to their room.

'Maybe we were always just too swept up by the excitement each summer that we never noticed all the things that were going wrong,' Marigold said to Mabel, relieved to see she looked equally concerned.

'Or maybe things really haven't been this bad before so no one's tried to fix it, but now . . .'

'Now what?' Mabel's voice trembled.

'I don't know.' Marigold shrugged. 'But I can't imagine it's very good.'

# 4

# Boys Don't Dance

'What do you want to be when you're older?'

It was only the first day of the summer holiday and the children were already bored of being asked that question. Marigold was now twelve years old, Mabel was ten and Morris was eight. Everyone seemed far more interested in their futures than they were. All the children could think about was the fact that they had a whole exciting summer to spend helping out Lydia backstage at the theatre. 'Would you all like to work in theatre when you're grown-up?' Petunia asked, leaning through the hatch of the little office at the stage door. She had to duck through on account of the purple witch's hat she was wearing, which came to a very tall, sharp point.

'I just want to write,' said Marigold, moving her coal-black hair away from her face to reveal a pencil tucked neatly behind her ear.

'You could write plays!' Petunia grinned.

'Maybe . . . but I think I'd prefer to write books.' Marigold's eyes lit up.

'Would you write any books about science?' asked Mabel.

'Ahh, we have a scientist in our midst!' Petunia's eyes flashed with interest. 'Biology? Chemistry?'

'Physics!' shouted Mabel. 'Space and time and . . .'

'Maths . . .' said Marigold, raising an eyebrow at her younger sister.

'Yes, all right, I'm not so good at the maths part yet, but I'm getting much better at my times tables, thank you very much.' Mabel was about to poke out her tongue but one sharp look from her older sister kept it firmly inside her mouth.

'What about young Morris, here?'

'Who knows?' Morris sighed.

'Nothing at school pique your interest?' Petunia probed, but Morris simply shrugged.

'Ahh! I know that feeling all too well. Sometimes it takes a little while to find something you love more than anything else, but when you find it . . .' Petunia took a long deep breath and she smiled with her eyes closed, as if she were smelling the sweetest rose. 'Bliss! Of course, I already know exactly what your futures hold.' Petunia flourished her tarot cards with a gleam in her eyes. 'But that would be telling!'

Cora also seemed to have a keen interest in the Pebbles' ambitions when they visited her and Layton.

'A writer, a scientist and a . . .' Cora paused when she got to Morris and he averted his gaze.

'Who knows?' Morris had found himself shrugging quite a lot since the summer holidays had begun.

'You'll figure it out sooner or later,' Cora said, with a reassuring pat on his shoulder.

'Can it be sooner, please?' Morris said and Cora laughed, a little awkwardly, but she didn't have much other encouragement to offer except a kind smile. When she closed the door, Morris turned to his sisters.

'How do you both know what you want to be when you're older?' This time, Marigold and Mabel both shrugged.

'It's just a . . . a feeling, I suppose,' said Marigold.

'There's really nothing you love doing? Nothing that makes you excited?' asked Mabel, and Morris thought really hard. Nothing sprang to mind. Nothing at all, and his cheeks began to burn.

'It really doesn't matter, Morris!' Marigold said gently.

'Yeah, Morris, you're the youngest! We didn't know what we wanted to be when we were your age either.' Mabel put her hand on Morris's shoulder but he pulled away and began to walk in the opposite direction.

'Where are you going?' Marigold shouted after him.

'I just want to be left alone,' Morris called over his shoulder but, as he turned back, he ran straight into the tree trunk-like legs of Theodore.

'Everything all right, lad?' Theodore looked down at Morris, whose expression was pulled tightly together in a frown. Morris was going to duck between Theodore's legs and make a dash for it, but instead he needed to know if it really was just him.

'Theo, when you were my age, did you know you were going to be a stuntman?'

'Goodness me! No! When I was your age, I wanted . . . well . . . to tell you the truth, Morris, I just wanted to dance.'

'A . . . dancer?' Theodore couldn't help but laugh at Morris's raised eyebrows.

'I know, I know. I'm definitely more suited to the job I have now, but when I was your age all I wanted to do was waltz and salsa and tap!'

'But . . . boys don't dance,' Morris said. Marigold and Mabel scoffed behind him and when he looked over his shoulder they both had their hands on their hips. He knew this was a sign he'd said something silly. 'Well, that's what Barry Miller always says at school!'

'Well, Barry Miller is a –'

'Language, Mabel!' Marigold interrupted, knowing her sister all too well.

'I was only going to say a ninny . . .' Mabel said, and she made her eyes big, round and innocent, but promptly followed with a wry smile.

'Barry Miller said what?!' boomed Theodore. 'But . . . what about . . . Come with me.' Theodore took Morris's hand and turned quickly in his big chunky boots and thumped down the corridor with Marigold and Mabel in tow. They went down a flight of stairs to stage level, where there were a few dressing rooms close by for those who needed to get to and from the stage very quickly when a performance was on. Theodore opened the door to his dressing room and ushered them all inside. It was cramped and unpainted with just a dressing table and a flimsy fold-out chair plonked against the wall. He flipped a switch, which illuminated the bulbs along the edges of the mirror so that Morris could see better. Stuck to the walls were pictures of dancers – mainly ballerinas, but also some tap dancers from famous movies like *Singin' in the Rain*, *Stormy Weather* and *Top Hat*. However, the thing Morris noticed straight away was that all the dancers were men.

'I was never much of a dancer myself. I was never a dancer at all, really,' said Theodore. 'I've always been too clumsy to live out that particular dream. My mum always said I was born with two left feet – but boy do I love watching other people who do it well. Fred Astaire, Gene Kelly, Bill

Robinson, the Nicholas Brothers . . . the best dancers this world has ever seen.'

Morris took in all the pictures. Men in top hats and tuxedos with tap shoes that glistened under the spotlights. Each dancer was surrounded by people who were smiling, cheering and applauding. No one seemed to look confused by the fact they were men who loved to dance.

'Barry Miller doesn't have a clue what he's talking about!' Theodore bellowed.

'No . . .' Morris said, gazing at one picture in particular of Bill Robinson in mid-air with a pair of gleaming tap shoes on his feet. 'No, I suppose he doesn't.'

Kitty and Claudia were the easiest to find of all the residents of the Pebble Theatre, because you could hear them either tapping or bickering from anywhere in the building. Morris was thankful to have found them in the front-of-house bar, away from where his sisters could hear what he wanted to ask. Kitty and Claudia had a large wooden board they could lay over the carpet so they could tap wherever and whenever they wanted. When Morris entered the bar, neither of them stopped tapping but their bobbing heads both turned to look at him.

'Look who it is, Kitty!'

'It's little Morris Pebble, Claudia!'

'Yes, I know who it is.'

'Then why did you ask me?'

'I didn't. I was just saying, Morris has come to see us.'

'Well, you could have just said that in the first place.'

'Hello, Fortune Sisters.' The Pebble children had learnt to cut through their squabbling quite quickly or it would never cease.

'It's rare you come to visit without your sisters, Master Morris.'

'How can we help you, Master Morris?' Their dancing slowed as they became more curious.

'I was wondering if maybe you had the time to . . . teach me how to dance?' Quite abruptly, the tapping stopped and the silence that filled the room was somehow even louder. 'Only if you have the time. I don't want to be any trouble. I just think . . . I dunno . . . I might . . . like it?'

'He's asking us to teach him to dance,' Kitty mumbled out of the side of her mouth to her sister.

'I know, Claudia, I have ears. I heard him,' Claudia mumbled back, neither of them taking their false-eyelashed eyes off him.

'We've never taught anyone before,' Kitty hissed.

'We taught ourselves and we're all right,' Claudia whispered.

'I'd only want to learn the basics for now,' Morris assured them. 'I'm a total beginner.'

'Only the basics. Total beginner,' they repeated.

'We can do that, can't we, Kitty?'

'I think we can, Claudia.'

'So . . . is that a yes?' Morris felt his heart skip a beat.

'WE'D LOVE TO!' Kitty and Claudia scuttled over to him and kissed him on both cheeks. They took his hands and guided him over to the board on the floor.

'Now, stand on one leg,' Kitty instructed.

'What? Like this?' Morris tentatively lifted one leg off the floor and instantly wobbled.

'Careful, now! That's it! Like a flamingo!' Claudia clapped as Morris regained his balance. 'Now, with the leg that's in the air, sort of . . . scuff the toe of your shoe back and forth on the board.'

'Like this?' Morris scuffed his trainer, and the rubber squeaked.

'That's it! Now, do it in time to my clapping.' Kitty began to clap-clap, clap-clap, clap-clap, clap-clap. It took Morris a few moments to find the right rhythm, but eventually his foot was perfectly in time with Kitty's claps.

'You're doing it!'

'I'm doing it!' Morris squeaked like his shoes.

'Now that, Master Morris, is called a "shuffle".'

'I'm shuffling?!'

'You're shuffling!'

'We'll teach you all kinds of little steps like that, then you can string them together to create longer dances. Sort of like how a writer knows lots of little words that they string together to tell stories!' said Kitty.

'Or how a scientist knows lots of little equations that they string together to solve some of the world's hardest puzzles!' said Claudia.

'I'm not sure dancing is as important as being an author or a scientist.' Doubt flashed across Morris's face and the Fortune Sisters exchanged a glance.

'We're going to write you a list.' Kitty grabbed a clean white napkin off the bar and Claudia took her freshly sharpened eyeliner out of her nearby bag.

'A list?' Morris asked, as they began to scribble, taking it in turns.

'Yes. A list of all the best movies starring all the best dancers,' Kitty explained.

'Movies that will make you laugh and cry and jump for joy!' Claudia actually jumped for joy.

'They'll make you feel like you can take on the entire world.' Kitty grinned as Claudia handed him the napkin.

'Then come back and tell us that dancing isn't important,' they said with a firm and final nod.

# 5

## In Mabel We Believe

Morris was now practising fervently with Kitty and Claudia every day, and his passion grew with every skilful shuffle of his foot and every perfect pirouette. He was very proud of his dancing and how quickly he was improving, especially after he'd been introduced to some classic musical movies. Morris watched and rewatched every single one until he had all the moves memorized. It wasn't long before Marigold and Mabel found out because, like the Fortune Sisters, you could hear him tappity-tapping wherever he was and it was rare that he didn't waltz into a room. Theodore had given Morris his old tap shoes from when he'd had lessons as a young boy.

He gladly handed them over to someone who would cherish them and give them the attention they deserved. Mack often tried to join in with Morris's dancing but Morris once accidentally stood on his tail so then Mack only watched Morris's feet, instead of getting under them. Once Morris had learnt all the moves, he danced along with the great dancers in the movies until his feet were so tired he would fall asleep with his tap shoes still on.

Mabel couldn't quite bring herself to congratulate him on his new-found hobby just yet. She didn't understand how he'd improved so much and so quickly! Mabel loved physics. This was the science of space and time. Every astronaut who had ever been into space had to pass all sorts of exams, including physics. While Mabel wasn't keen on the idea of going to space herself (she felt sick just riding on the bus!), the idea of sending someone or something into space excited her greatly. However, even though she enjoyed physics a great deal, a big part of the science was maths and Mabel was not very good at maths. No matter how hard she tried to make the numbers add up, her answers always seemed to be wrong – but she was scared of putting up her hand and asking for help at school. Her teacher never noticed she was struggling until after she'd handed her book in at the end of class and scurried off to the playground to pretend she was flying to the moon. When Mabel got her book back in the next class, she always opened it up hoping that maybe, this time, something had clicked in her head and she had finally got all the answers right. But, sadly, her book was always covered in red ink. She felt stupid and shy and the more she wanted to disappear and not have anyone notice how silly she felt, the more she felt bad. She'd shake her hair so that it half-hid her face from any onlookers. She only tied it back when Lydia made her at bedtime and, even then, she would want the light turned out immediately.

'Why don't you say something?' asked Marigold, when Mabel had finally told her why she was crying. Mabel lay in her bed, in the dark, letting her tears spill quietly down the sides of her cheeks and on to her pillow. Marigold could tell Mabel was upset because Mack was curled up at the bottom of her bed. Mabel hadn't noticed and Marigold wasn't going to tell her. It was the perfect way to judge her sister's mood.

'I'm stupid.' Mabel sobbed. 'People will make fun of me because I can't do the sums.'

Marigold sniffed hard. It was times like this when Marigold wished that Bam was better at using her mobile phone. Bam was extremely good at boosting morale and giving personal pep talks just when you needed them. What Marigold wouldn't give to be able to dial her number and pass the phone over to Mabel. She'd be smiling in no time. *What would Brilliant Aunt Maude say?* Marigold thought.

'Mabel Pebble,' Marigold said, trying to sound as much like Bam as she could. 'Don't you dare say such a mean thing about yourself.' Morris stirred at her raised voice and Mabel hushed her riled sister. Marigold sat up in bed and, although it was pitch-black and Mabel couldn't see her, Mabel knew Marigold was giving her one of her scary serious sisterly stares. 'If I had told you I was stupid, what would you say?'

Mabel went quiet for a moment. 'I'd be sad you were talking about yourself like that. You're betterer than everyone in your class!'

'It's just better,' Marigold corrected.

'Huh?' Mabel sniffed.

'Never mind. Now you know how it makes me feel to hear you talk about yourself like that. You may not be clever when it comes to numbers but that's something you can learn over time. You're better at other things and clever in other ways.'

'Am I?'

'Do you remember when we were all allowed to wear Halloween costumes to school last year, and all three of us forgot? You dragged us all into the toilets at once, wrapped us up in toilet paper, and we all went as mummies. We would have won the best-dressed competition if Tony Mullins hadn't come in actual bandages!'

Mabel sniffed hard in the dark.

'And that time we got locked out but you could see Theodore's spare set of keys through the window and, although the window was open, none of us could fit through it. Do you remember? You had a spare magnet in your school bag and you used it to move the keys up the glass and out of the open window. It was genius!' Mabel giggled. 'See? You might not be good at the number stuff *yet* but you're very good at problem-solving and NASA needs a lot of problem-solvers.' Marigold heard Mabel shift under her covers and sit up in her bed.

'Do you really think I could do it? Make it to NASA, I mean?' Mabel whispered.

'Definitely! *But* only if you work hard.'

'I will!' Mabel said with certainty.

'*And* you ask for help when you need it. Even if you think people will think you're stupid. Which you're not, by the way, but the others at school might make fun of you for asking questions. Admitting you don't understand something sounds like you're being stupid but it's actually a very clever thing to do.'

'It doesn't feel very clever,' Mabel huffed.

'*And* only if you believe in yourself. Believe in yourself as much as Morris and I believe in you.'

Mabel lay down again and went quiet. And, just when Marigold thought she'd finally drifted off to sleep, she whispered, 'You believe in me, Marigold?'

'Of course I do. You're my sister.' Marigold lay down. A tiny voice drifted through the darkness.

'Marigold?'

'Yes, Mabel,' Marigold said through a yawn.

'How did *you* get to be so clever?'

'*Ahh*, that's a special Big Sister thing. No matter how clever you are, I will always be betterer.'

'It's just better.'

'Exactly.' Marigold smiled and fell swiftly asleep.

# 6

# The Voice Inside Marigold's Head

Morris and Mabel were very lucky to have an older sister like Marigold. She never really said much unless you asked her questions, in which case she always had an answer – and more often than not she was right. Marigold liked to *observe* (which is just a fancy word for watch) but she would watch *very* closely. She observed the people around her and had become very good at reading faces. She could sometimes tell what people were thinking before they even knew it themselves, and sometimes what they said didn't match what Marigold thought they were thinking. This meant she could spot a liar. Mabel and Morris learnt very quickly that they couldn't get away with anything, because nothing got past Marigold. It was best to just be honest in the first place. Marigold also had an excellent memory and an even better imagination, so she didn't really *have* to say anything much because there was always plenty going on in her head. This didn't make her popular at school. While Marigold was probably the most academic of the Pebble children, she was also intelligent beyond her years in ways the other children weren't. She was enthusiastic about learning, which the other children were not. They laughed when she raised her hand before the teacher had even finished asking the question, and they sniggered when Marigold always offered to help. She also had buckets of something called 'empathy'. When someone picked on Morris at school, it made Marigold cry too because she knew just how badly Morris must be feeling. When she was reading at lunchtime, she sometimes had to close the book for fear of her heart breaking at a particularly sad ending. She fed off the feelings of those around her and Lydia had noticed this. She couldn't have been more grateful for Marigold's sensible and responsible disposition, especially when Mabel and Morris were both larger than life. However, Lydia did worry that Marigold bottled up all her feelings and she feared what might happen if they began to overflow – especially if she had no friends to talk to.

On the second day of their summer holidays, Marigold decided to get stuck in with theatre chores. She was helping

Lydia organize boxes in a spare dressing room that was used to store odds and ends that had no other home. Scripts, scores, props and old costumes – some were as old as Bam herself. Marigold pretended she liked to help tidy, but really she just liked looking through the theatre's history and seeing what would spark her imagination. Sometimes Lydia would insist on getting rid of something, only for it to end up on Marigold's bedside table. Mabel and Morris had politely declined the invitation to spring clean, and so Lydia took this opportunity to make sure Marigold was as happy and carefree as she should be.

'You don't ever worry about anything other than what you should be worrying about, do you?' Marigold looked at Lydia, trying to read her expression, but Lydia kept her head in a script for *Oklahoma*, slowly flipping through the pages even though she knew every line by heart.

'What *should* I be worrying about?' Marigold asked, and Lydia sighed.

'Well, you shouldn't be worrying about anything, really! But sometimes you're so quiet, Marigold. As if you're carrying the weight of the world on your shoulders.'

'I just think a lot, that's all.' Marigold shrugged.

'What do you think about?' Lydia asked gently.

Marigold thought for a moment. 'About the world, I suppose, and everyone in it.' It was the answer Lydia had expected but Marigold said it with such lightness, as if all twelve-year-olds carried the world inside their heads all the time.

'The world is quite large, Marigold. That's an awful lot to fit inside one young mind.'

Lydia was beginning to worry if maybe this were too big a conversation, when Marigold said, 'Planet Earth is very small compared to all the other worlds I think about.'

'Other worlds?' Lydia raised an eyebrow.

'Yes. All the worlds I'm going to write about one day and all the people who live in them.' Marigold became very animated as she spoke and a smile spread across her face, bigger than Lydia had ever seen. 'Not to mention all the worlds I've already read about! Like Narnia and Wonderland, Hobbiton and Hogwarts! One day, I'm going to write about my own world and everyone's going to read it and want to live there.'

Lydia felt a weight lift off her shoulders. Marigold wasn't quiet because something was wrong. She was quiet because so much was right. She was quiet because she was stocking up on information and inspiration so that one day she could turn it into something magical to unleash on the world. A huge rush of pride flushed through her.

'Why wait?' Lydia said, blinking her tears away.

'What?'

'You said "one day" you're going to write about your own world, but why wait to write when you're already so capable now?' Lydia pulled another box towards her and pulled out a notebook that had been used in a production of *Little Women*.

'I'm too young! I don't know enough! No one writes novels when they're twelve!'

'You can!' Lydia held out the notebook to her. 'Besides, lots of authors started young. Mary Shelley was only eighteen when she wrote *Frankenstein*. Anne Frank was only a year older than you when she started her diary, and it's one of the most important books ever written! You have every chance of being as brilliant as they were. You just have to give it a go.' To Lydia, it was just a notebook – but to Marigold it was a hundred blank pages. A hundred chances to get it wrong. A hundred chances to write the worst book the world has ever read.

'I can't.' Marigold shook her head, the fire in her dimming.

'Who says?' Lydia scoffed.

'Me,' Marigold said weakly.

'Ah.' And there it was. Morris had kids at school telling him dancing wasn't for boys. Maths was squashing Mabel's dreams. But it was Marigold herself that was holding Marigold back. It was the voice inside her own head that was telling her: '*No. You're not good enough. You can't do it.*'

'What if the story I write is terrible?' Marigold said, looking down at her hands.

'How will you know, if you don't ever write anything?' Lydia flapped the book about in front of her, hoping Marigold would take the bait.

'But —'

'Marigold,' Lydia said, lowering the book but keeping a firm hold of it. 'If, and only IF, what you write is terrible, then you keep writing until it's a little bit *less* terrible. Then you keep writing until it is actually quite good. Then you keep putting your pen to that paper and you write and write and write until you're ninety-two, you've written three hundred books, and the whole world knows not only your name but your stories, too.' Marigold was quiet. Lydia thought maybe she'd pushed a little too hard and so she lay the notebook to rest in her lap and returned to the task at hand.

'Do you really think I could do it? Write a whole book one day?' Marigold said quietly. Lydia let out a small sigh, swivelled herself round to face Marigold and took hold of both her hands.

'Marigold,' Lydia said with a smile. 'It shouldn't matter what I or anyone else thinks. The question is, do *you* think you can do it?'

'I . . . don't know, Lydia.' Marigold sighed.

Lydia lifted the book and held it out to Marigold one last time. 'Find out.'

Marigold took the notebook and Lydia saw a glimmer of hope in Marigold's eyes that suddenly faded.

'OK, but . . . can I pick a different notebook? This one's a bit . . . grotty.'

Lydia laughed. 'Yes, of course. There's a box of them in the corner. Old props and whatnot. Some might have pages missing, or messages scribbled by actors who were probably pretending to write important documents on stage — but take your pick! Most will go in the bin and the nicer ones to a charity shop, which is where these thirty scores for *The Sound of Music* will go!' Lydia dragged the box, which was far too heavy to lift, out of the room and Marigold went to rummage around for something more suitable for a young writer.

When she looked in the box in the corner, she only saw Mack the cat lazily curled up on a pile of books. As she shifted the box he stretched and yawned, which turned into a meow of annoyance as Marigold gently tipped the box on its side. Mack tumbled out of the box along with several notebooks. With a little hiss, he sauntered from the room. Most of the notebooks, while covered in ginger fur, were large. They were far too big for Marigold to fit in her rucksack. They were ledgers from shows with bookkeeping roles, shop owners, accountants and the like. Even though they weren't what Marigold was looking for she thumbed through them anyway, spotting the odd page midway through each mostly blank book where an actor had written a note to another actor. There were only three or four notebooks that were of a decent size. She piled them up and took them over to an empty desk, where she dumped them with a thud, a cloud of dust billowing up from their yellowing covers. Each desk in the theatre came with a mirror lined with lightbulbs and this one was no different, even though it hadn't been used in years. Marigold flicked the switch and with a buzz they slowly lit up. Most of them did, anyway. A few of them flickered and died, and two of them didn't come on at all – but enough of them worked for Marigold to be able to inspect the notebooks much better. As she sat with a thud, one of the books slid from the desk on to the floor and a few of its pages came loose and scattered.

'Well, I won't be using that one. Too fragile,' she muttered as she knelt to pick it up. But, as she shuffled the pages back into the book's cover, she noticed something on the underside of the dressing-room desk. There was a little hole in the wall and plaster had crumbled away into a pile on the carpet. Marigold would have swept it up and thought nothing of it – it was just a bit of an old theatre eroding over time – if she hadn't spotted, peeping out of the hole, a little folded piece of newspaper. The date was displayed clearly: 24 September 1946. Marigold shuffled closer and, with a trembling breath, reached her hand into the hole. She had a sudden vision of something on the other side of the wall grabbing her arm and sucking her into the theatre, never to be seen again – or worse . . . a mouse crawling across her palm! A wave of panic made her shudder, so Marigold grabbed whatever lay inside the hole and whipped it out. The object hit the floor with a bump. It was a brown envelope, opened at one end where the newspaper stuck out. On the envelope was the address of the Pebble Theatre and lots of postmarks she didn't recognize, but the large stamp in the corner had a picture of the Empire State Building on it. *America!* she thought with excitement. *Is that where it came from?* When she first glanced into the envelope, it looked like it could just be a folded-up newspaper but, when Marigold gave it a squeeze, she could tell that the paper was wrapped around something rigid at the centre. Something exciting, she hoped. But one thing she did know was that there was absolutely no way she was going to open it without Mabel and Morris.

# 7

# A Blast from the Past

'It could be filled with . . . human teeth!' Morris yelled, gnashing his teeth together and running to Marigold's bed.

'Or . . . it could be filled with buttons and cotton wool!' Marigold rolled her eyes. 'We don't know.' She had hidden the parcel under her jumper all the way up to the top of the theatre and stuffed it under her mattress. It wasn't that she liked keeping secrets, quite the opposite in fact. Marigold hated lying, even if it was only a little lie, but, whatever this package contained, something told her it was for her and her siblings – and them alone. Their eyes only. She promised herself that she would tell Lydia where she'd found it and that she'd taken it without asking *after* they discovered exactly what it was. Surely no one would miss it? It had been under a desk and behind a wall for who knows how many years.

'Well, why are we all just staring at it?' said Mabel, catapulting herself from her bed to Marigold's. Lydia had long since tucked them in for bedtime, and when all the lights were out Marigold had confessed to her sneaky goings-on and let her brother and sister in on her secret. They daren't turn on the big light so Mabel unravelled the fairy lights from the end of her bed and, keeping them plugged in and turned on, bundled them on to the bed. Then she grabbed her quilt, wafted it up into the air above their heads and quickly ducked under it herself. With all three of them huddled warmly in the darkness, with only tiny, twinkling bulbs in the middle of the circle to light their conversation, the atmosphere for secret sibling shenanigans was perfect. 'Aren't we going to open it?' Mabel snatched up the parcel and shook it.

'Careful!' Marigold said, taking it back.

'At least we can rule out buttons. It doesn't rattle,' Mabel said, after poking out her tongue.

'Teeth too, then.' Morris pouted. 'Could be a pair of tap shoes, though?'

'Not heavy enough,' Marigold said, feeling the weight of it in her hands.

'Or big enough. How about a chemistry set?' Mabel's eyes sparkled.

'Don't think so. I think . . . I think it might be a book.'

'A book?' Mabel said with an exaggerated yawn.

'Goodnight!' Morris stuck his head out from under the quilt, ready to leave their little bubble, but Marigold gently took his hand in hers.

'Books are better than tap shoes and chemistry sets,' Marigold said quietly.

'No, they're not!' Morris protested.

'They're just dead trees full of words,' Mabel said, beginning to untangle herself from the fairy lights.

'They're not. They're forests full of stories. You can get entirely lost in the pages of a book and be whoever and *whatever* you want to be. You could be a dancer or a scientist right now if you picked up the right book.' Marigold looked down at the parcel, feeling its edges between her fingers. She could feel where the spine met the cover and the thickness of its pages.

'Well, if books are all *that* – prove it,' Mabel said.

'Yeah. Let's open it,' said Morris.

'Together?' Marigold smiled.

'Together.' Her brother and sister smiled back. Marigold slid the newspaper-wrapped object from the envelope. There was a string secured round it like a present, which Morris tried to untie, but it was so old it came loose in his hands with ease. He unwrapped the first layer of newspaper, Mabel unwrapped the next and Marigold unwrapped the last to find that she was right. It *was* a book. The hard cover was green, and two beautiful letters shone in gold foil in the centre.

'PF?' whispered Marigold, tracing the letters with the tip of her finger. The newspaper wrapping had made sure it didn't get dusty, but it looked like it had been opened and closed a thousand times. The spine was cracked in many different places and the edges of the cover were frayed and grubby. Whoever owned the book must have read it over and over and over again. However, when Morris flipped open the cover, they discovered that it was a book unlike any they had ever seen. Written on the first page was this:

*We three Fossils vow to try to put our names in history books because it's our very own and nobody can say it's because of our grandfathers.*

Underneath, three girls had signed their names. Pauline first, in beautiful cursive handwriting, then a few spots of ink dappled the 'P' in Petrova's name, and finally Posy was written in large, precise capitals.

'Pauline, Petrova and Posy. Who are they?' Marigold asked. All of the signatures looked so different from each other, yet they all overlapped somewhere. Pauline's curly signature intertwined with the 't' in 'Petrova' and the ink splattered across Petrova's name spilt down into the 'o' of Posy. All so individual, yet all linked.

'They certainly didn't get *that* famous then, did they? I've never heard of them!' scoffed Mabel.

'Now hang on a minute!' When Marigold's voice was stern like that she sounded almost exactly like Lydia. It made both Morris's and Mabel's backs stiffen. 'They didn't want to become famous. They wanted to get their names in history books.' Marigold read the vow once more in her head to make sure she'd got that right.

'Yeah? So? What's the difference?' Mabel folded her arms.

'There are lots of people throughout history who did amazing things. Things you wouldn't believe! People who have saved thousands of lives and helped millions more. People who proved themselves to be heroes and yet no one knows about them. Maybe Pauline, Petrova and Posy *are* in the history books, but they're not names that everyone knows.'

'So what's the point in doing anything then, if no one knows about it?' said Mabel.

'Ask Morris.' Marigold looked at her brother.

'Me? What have I done?!' Morris shrieked.

'Morris, I'm going to give you a choice. Either you become a dancer for the rest of your life, in big Broadway shows and maybe even in movies . . . but no one remembers your name. Or you become famous for something else, but you can never dance again. At all. Ever. Which do you choose?' Marigold put her nose in the air, knowing her brother well enough to know what he'd reply.

'The dancing one,' Morris said quickly, because for him it

really was the simplest choice in the world. 'Never put on a pair of tap shoes again? Never do a pirouette in my whole entire life? Are you joking? I'd rather no one ever knew my name or my face than give up dancing.' He shuddered at the thought.

'See?' Marigold turned back to Mabel, who was slightly pink in the face. 'Surely you'd be happy putting a hundred people into space in *your* rockets, with *your* science, and never getting any recognition, than never becoming a physicist at all . . . right?' Mabel thought for a moment, finding it very hard to admit that her big sister was correct, but finally she nodded.

'Yeah, I suppose you're right.' Mabel unfolded her arms and fiddled with the scrunched-up newspaper the volume had been wrapped in.

'It doesn't look like a *proper* book . . . so what is it?' asked Morris, peering over the first page.

'I think it's a . . . a journal.' Marigold grinned, but as she was about to turn the page Mabel put her hand over Marigold's fingers.

'Wait, a *what*?'

Marigold sighed as she was desperate to turn the page, but she also knew that these special kinds of moments mustn't be rushed. 'Sort of like a diary but less . . . private. And usually you put other things in journals.'

'Like what?' asked Morris, his eyebrows knitting together.

'Like memories. From places you've been to or photographs of people you never want to forget.'

'So, these three people kept a journal? Together?' asked Morris, shifting himself so he was now hugging his knees to his chest.

'Looks like it. They all have the same last name. See? Fossil. They must have been sisters.'

'That's a really weird last name,' muttered Mabel.

Marigold tutted and said, 'No weirder than Pebble.'

'I like it,' said Morris with a smile. 'It sounds old-school. Anyone with a name like that was bound to make it into the history books.'

'We still don't even know if they *did* make it into the history books,' said Mabel, with a roll of her eyes. Morris ignored his sister's negativity.

'Let's read it!' he whispered.

'Isn't that a bit . . . rude? Reading someone else's diary?' Marigold bit her lip.

'You already said it's not a diary. It's a journal. Besides, it was written in the 1940s. I doubt any of them are still about to be annoyed at us,' said Mabel.

'How do you know that?'

'The newspaper.' Mabel held up the scrap of newspaper they had unwrapped only moments ago.

'Of course! Mabel, you're a genius!' Marigold said, remembering.

'I am?'

Marigold took the newspaper from her clever sister and there, plain as day, right in the corner, was the date. '24 September 1946. That must have been the day one of these three sisters hid the journal in the theatre. She wrapped it up in that day's newspaper and tucked it out of sight. Like a time capsule.'

'And it's been there ever since? No one ever found it?' Morris said, scooting closer to Marigold to get a better look.

'Doesn't look like it,' Mabel whispered, leaning in closer, too.

'Until now.' And finally, with a deep breath, Marigold turned the page.

Pauline, Petrova and Posy *were* sisters. Not because they had the same mother and father but because fate had intervened and placed them together in the care of their great-uncle Matthew.

'That's just like us!' Mabel gasped. 'They were sisters because the universe made them so,' she added with a nod. The first entry in the journal was written in 1939 and came from Pauline, the eldest, who had left to become a Hollywood actress. Petrova, whose entry came next, went with her great-uncle Matthew to be a pilot and Posy, the youngest, left to go to Czechoslovakia to . . .

'. . . become a dancer!' Morris grabbed the journal to get a better look at the newspaper cutting. All the writing was in a different language so he couldn't understand it, but right in the centre was a photograph of a young girl in ballet tights, a leotard and a beautiful tutu being lifted into the air by a man. *They both look so strong*, he thought.

'Don't hog it!' Mabel playfully pushed her brother's shoulder. 'Are there any pictures of Petrova?'

'Well, let's not skip ahead,' Marigold said sternly.

'It's not a story, Marigold.' Mabel laughed.

'Well, it kind of *is*. It's the story of the Fossils and their travels around the world. It's *their* story, which is just as important as any other, isn't it?'

'So, should we read it like a book, then?' asked Morris, with a raised eyebrow.

'I think that's the best way, don't you?' Marigold held out her hand for the book, but Morris had already begun flipping through the first few pages.

'Look! They all write an entry and then pass it on. Pauline, then Petrova, then Posy – and then round again.' Morris passed it to his big sister.

'They must have begun to miss each other so much they wrote to each other in this journal!' Marigold held the book close to her face to get a better look at the photo.

'That explains the stamp and the strange postmarks on the envelope. It must have come from Posy in New York.' Morris's mouth fell open.

'Which means, it came to . . . to Pauline, here at the Pebble

Theatre.' Marigold traced the initials on the cover with the tip of her finger.

'But that means . . . she must have performed here,' said Mabel.

'*Here?*' Marigold gasped.

'On *our* stage?' Morris grinned.

'Before we were even born.' Mabel laughed. Morris began to fidget as though he had electricity running through his limbs.

'Oh, Marigold, we have to read it, we just *have* to! Dibs on reading Posy's bits!' Morris said, shooting his hand into the air.

'I want to read the pilot's entries!' Mabel shouted.

'Shhhhh! Lydia will hear us!' Marigold hushed them.

'Why do you want to be the pilot?' Morris asked, his nose scrunched in confusion.

'Pilots always have a big sense of adventure! They like to explore the unknown,' Mabel replied, looking up towards the sky. Even though they were under a quilt, she'd looked up at the night sky enough times to be able to see it in her mind. 'Plus, I reckon I'll need some knowledge of flying before I send people into space when I'm older. Maybe Petrova has some handy tips.' She shrugged.

'The book starts with Pauline. I suppose I'm reading for her?' said Marigold. Mabel and Morris nodded, their heads casting bobbing shadows against the quilt in the fairy lights. 'OK. Let's all take a deep breath and calm down a moment.'

Mabel shut her eyes tight and did as she was told, but Morris's breath squeaked as he breathed in, which made them all giggle.

'OK, OK. Here we go.' Marigold turned the pages back to the beginning and began to read . . .

*11 June 1939*

*Dearest Petrova and Posy,*

*I trust you are both well and behaving yourselves as you should be. Los Angeles is not at all what I expected. It's so . . . big! But not like London is big, with its looming buildings and millions of people pushing their way down Oxford Street in one big clump — Los Angeles is spread out. It's vast. You can drive for miles and miles, past beaches and palm trees, and still not be where you need to be. There's no hopping on the 65 bus from Cromwell Road and ten minutes later you're at your final destination. I miss London for that.*

*Sylvia is doing well. The warm temperature seems to agree with her. She looks happier too, even though she's not quite accustomed to all the fussing people seem to do on film sets. I wish you both could see it, although you'd both laugh, no doubt. Seeing people spend hours doing my make-up and lacing me into corsets, only for me to forget my lines in the*

first take! How embarrassing! Sylvia gave me quite a telling-
off and now she makes me go over my scenes every night.
Rightly so.

Petrova, how's the air up there? Whenever I look to the
sky I think of you, gliding about in your big metal birds.

Posy, how are your feet? Not too sore, I hope!

I never said it enough before I left, but I am so very proud
of you both. Of us all. The history books are calling!

Sending love,
Pauline

# 8

# The History Books

It was a twenty-minute walk to the nearest library in Pimlico. Lydia usually took them twice a month on a Saturday morning during term time, but now that it was the summer holidays, she was happy to take them as often as they liked. However, she would insist that they take out two books each and return them, having read them both, on their next visit. Marigold loved to read so much that she often begged Lydia to let her take out five books, which was the most you were allowed to have, but Lydia knew how often things went missing in the theatre and didn't want to be facing any library fines. However, she loved Marigold's enthusiasm for reading and so allowed her to take out one more book than her younger siblings. Mabel and Morris were fine with this. It wasn't that they disliked reading, it was just that their interests were different. When Mabel checked books out of the library, they were about space and science, and Morris often took home books about Broadway shows and autobiographies written by dancers. He liked the pictures more than anything. This visit to the library, however, was a little different. On the walk there they all talked to each other a little more quietly than usual.

'What are you three up to? I'm usually having to tell you all to use your inside voices because your outside voices are too loud – even when we're outside!' Lydia ran to catch up with them, but they all stopped dead and turned to face her. Marigold had the journal in her rucksack, and she could feel it burning against her back. All of a sudden, she felt all hot under the collar of her red coat and she was certain Lydia knew something was going on.

'We're not up to anything, Lydia,' Mabel said, twirling her long hair round her fingers.

'Nothing at all!' said Morris, shuffling his feet.

'And what about you, Marigold?' Lydia said, her eyebrows raised, clearly unimpressed by their secrecy. Marigold was desperate to tell Lydia everything, not only because finding the journal was maybe the most exciting thing to happen to the Pebble children in the history of forever, but also because keeping the secret of the journal made Marigold feel hot and flustered and ever so nervous whenever she was around Lydia. But it had to remain a secret for now, until they'd found out who Pauline, Petrova and Posy were and whether they really did make the history books. Marigold was sure that Lydia would be so impressed that she would eventually forgive her for taking something that wasn't hers. Marigold swallowed hard and smiled wider than she normally would.

'I'm always quiet.' She shrugged.

'Hmm,' said Lydia, her eyebrows falling into their usual worried frown. 'Well, remember, you can always tell me anything. Anything at all.'

'We *know*,' they said together before they turned away and continued on to the library, whispering as they went.

Pimlico library wasn't fancy but it was quite big, and had shelves upon shelves of books – many of which Marigold had already read – but she'd never come across Pauline, Petrova or Posy. That didn't mean they weren't to be found somewhere in among the library's pages, but it did make her worry that their trip might be wasted. She didn't want to have to wait another two weeks before they came back for their next visit to look again. They stepped through the doors and, while Lydia was distracted chatting with the librarian on the front desk, Marigold rallied her troops.

'Are we clear on the plan? Mabel, your job . . . ?'

'. . . is to head to books about aerodynamics, female pilots and anything to do with planes.' Mabel nodded.

'Morris, your job . . . ?'

'. . . is to find anything written by famous ballet dancers and maybe even books about Czechoslovakia in the 1930s and 1940s.'

'And I'm going to see what I can find on the Pebble Theatre and Hollywood in the 1930s and 1940s. Meet me back here in half an hour. *Go!*' she said a little too enthusiastically, and two readers behind them, plus the librarian and Lydia, all turned to them and said *shush!*

Morris quickly flipped through all the books the library had that were written by dancers or about dancers. Most of the books had a section of pictures on glossy paper in the centre and so he found it easier to flip through them first, but he couldn't find Posy anywhere. Mabel's head became fuzzy looking through books about aeroplane engineering. There were so many big words and confusing drawings, she quickly felt her hope disappearing. Marigold, however, a girl who was very familiar with the library, was able to find a book about small theatres in London. The Pebble Theatre was near the end of the book, but sadly there was nothing about Pauline Fossil. She collected a pile of books she thought might be of use and sat at one of the tables, turning hundreds of pages by the minute. Finally, in a book about famous Hollywood film studios, Marigold found a black-and-white photograph of a 'wrap party'.

'When they say a film is "wrapped" that means they've finished filming it. This must be a photo from when they were celebrating!' Marigold showed her brother and sister what she had found.

'So?' Mabel shrugged, not really looking at the photo. Marigold rolled her eyes and pushed the book further under her sister's nose.

'Look at the names underneath. It's a list of all the people in the photo, from left to right. You can't really see her because she's sandwiched between so many other people, but, look!' Marigold put the tip of her finger just under the chin of a girl in the centre of the group huddled together. 'See? Near the back. Underneath it says it's Pauline Fossil. It's one of the sisters!' Mabel pulled the book towards her, and Marigold took great delight in seeing her eyes widen at the sight of the girl they had been reading about.

'She's so . . . *beautiful*!' Mabel gasped.

'But what about Posy?' Morris sulked.

'And Petrova,' cried Mabel, closing the book and handing it back.

'Can I help you three? You look like you're hunting for something in particular.' A woman in a pair of shiny green heels clip-clopped towards them. She seemed around the same age as Lydia but she was much thinner and taller, with bright piercing-blue eyes that shone through square glasses and red curls that were pinned up in a messy bun at the back of her head. Her black dress swished round her knees as she walked towards them.

'You've got red hair,' Mabel breathed.

'Yes, I have!' The woman laughed. 'And so do you! Do you like having red hair?' Mabel shook her head, unable to find her voice.

'You don't?' Marigold looked at her younger sister, who was now hiding behind the very hair she claimed to dislike. 'You've never said so before.'

'It's not that I don't like it. It's just . . . the girls at school tease me. They say people with red hair are always hot-headed and so they never let me play in case I lose my temper.' Mabel's bottom lip almost began to wobble but she took a deep breath before she let herself get emotional.

'Oh, for goodness' sake.' The woman rolled her eyes and crouched down so she could get a better look at Mabel's hidden eyes. 'I hated my hair when I was younger, too. Kids can be mean. But as you grow up, I promise you, you'll know people who actually pay lots of money to have someone dye their hair exactly your shade of red because they think it looks amazing. I've had more people tell me how jealous they are of my hair than I can count on my fingers and toes. Sure, there are people who will make the odd comment, but it's water off a ginger duck's back, my love.' The woman smiled.

'People actually pay to make their hair ginger?' Mabel sniffed.

'They do, indeed. They want to look like Ron Weasley or Amy Pond or . . . or . . . Prince Harry!'

Mabel threw her head back to laugh and her beautiful hair fell away from her face.

'There you are!' The woman sighed.

'Who are you, anyway?' Mabel said, wiping her nose on her sleeve and finding a little of her confidence once more.

'I'm Lady. I'm the new head librarian!'

'Lady,' Mabel repeated and then went awfully silent.

'This is my sister Mabel.' Morris stepped in, his hand held out for her to shake. 'I'm Morris.' Lady looked from Marigold to Mabel to Morris and back again.

'We're adopted,' Marigold explained.

'Yet you all smile the same.' Lady's eyes sparkled as she stood up to her normal height, towering over Marigold (and Marigold was the second-tallest girl in her class). 'Right! What can I help you with?' Lady clapped her hands together, ready for action.

'Nothing. We're OK,' said Morris, beginning to retreat back into the bookshelves.

'Actually, Morris,' said Marigold, 'we need help now more than ever. We're looking for three people in particular. They may have made the history books but, then again, they may have not. We don't know. Which is what we're trying to find out.'

'And you've been looking for them in all the books?' Lady raised an eyebrow, and all three Pebbles nodded.

'Well, that is like trying to find a needle in a haystack!' Lady shook her head.

'Three needles, in fact. In many possible haystacks,' said Marigold, looking about the thousands of books that surrounded them.

'May I suggest using one of the library's computers? They're state of the art and I bet if there are answers out there, they're on the internet.' Lady pointed over to the window where there were three or four sleek, expensive-looking computers. A couple of people were working at them, headphones on, their brows furrowed in hard concentration. The Pebble children loved using computers but had never used the fancy computers in the library. There was one very ancient computer at the stage door and another at the box office, both second-hand, but Bam said they weren't to be used for anything other than what they were bought for. The computers at school were quite old too, and they were only allowed on them for school exercises. The internet was only to be used under strict supervision after a few children typed some rude words into the search engine and got quite a shock!

'Please will you show us?' Marigold asked politely.

'Follow me.' Lady smiled and led the way. 'The internet is just a place for all the knowledge the human race currently has. There's a lot that's fact and there's a lot that's fiction, and sometimes one is disguised as the other and it's very hard to tell which one is which.'

'. . . I'm confused.' Morris scratched his head.

'Yes, I think I've confused myself.' Lady laughed. 'Let's start with what we came here for, shall we? What were those names, Marigold?' Lady sat down at one of the shiny computers and started it up. It made a '*bing bong*' noise, and the Pebbles gathered round Lady to get a closer look.

'Pauline, Petrova and Posy,' Marigold said slowly, watching Lady's hands tap quickly at the letters on the keyboard. Lady paused before she hit the return key.

'You mean the Fossil sisters?' she said.

'You know who they are?!' Mabel gasped.

'I only really know about Petrova Fossil, the pilot, but the other two were very bright and brilliant young women in their own spheres. One was a movie star and the other a ballerina. In the ballet in Prague, I think.'

'Yes, *we* know who they are. We found their −' Mabel began, but one quick glance from Marigold silenced her mid-sentence.

'We . . . we have found their history quite interesting!' stuttered Marigold. 'We . . . umm . . . we need to write an essay on each of the sisters. For school. I'm writing about Pauline, Mabel is writing about Petrova, and Morris is writing about Posy.' Marigold nodded so much, Mabel thought her head was going to topple off her shoulders, and her eyes were so wide, Morris thought they might pop out of her head.

'What's the essay about?' Lady asked. The cogs in Marigold's head spun faster and faster.

'Inspiring women!' she said.

'Well, in that case, you've certainly picked three brilliant women. It's just a shame more people don't know about them.'

'Why don't they?' asked Morris.

'I'm not sure. Some people make ripples and others make waves, but either way we are all part of the same ocean.'

'What do you know about Petrova?' Mabel jumped up and down, unable to contain her excitement. She was desperate to find out all she could about someone so clever.

'Now, let me think.' Lady rubbed her chin with her fingers. 'Petrova was probably the closest to making waves. She started by fixing up Spitfires during the Second World War with a man . . . oh, what was his name again? I can't remember now but he was a mechanic, too.'

'She was a mechanic?'

'Yes, at first, but she had a keen interest in learning to fly planes. When she was eighteen, she became part of the Air Transport Auxiliary during the Second World War. ATA-girls they used to call them. Women who had been trained to fly Spitfires, Harvards, Hurricanes and lots of other types of aircraft, so they could deliver them to airfields and sometimes even to front-line squadrons.'

'Women flew planes in the war?' Mabel's mouth dropped open.

'They did! She was one of one hundred and sixty-eight female pilots. There were, however, lots of people who didn't like the idea that women could do the jobs of men but Petrova was ahead of her time. She certainly showed them how it was done!' The children were completely entranced so Lady continued, digging in the corners of her brain for everything she knew about Petrova Fossil. 'It was quite a dangerous job, too! Fifteen women lost their lives in accidents, and for a while they thought Petrova was one of them. Her plane went down in a storm and she went missing.'

'What happened?' Morris asked.

'She found her way home, back to her sisters.'

'*Woooooaaaahhh*,' Mabel breathed.

'*Woah* indeed.' Lady nodded.

'Why don't we know about her if she was so brilliant?' Mabel pouted.

'There are lots of people who go unrecognized for the work they do, but I bet Petrova would say that it's not about getting praise or fame. It's about mucking in and doing what's right.' Lady let that thought hang for a moment before she clapped her hands together again. 'Shall we do some research?' She waved her finger in the air and then jabbed it at the 'Enter' button and the children leant in as the screen changed.

'*Ta-da!*' she announced, and was promptly shushed by

someone reading close by. 'Sorry!' she whispered. 'Four hundred thousand different entries about the Fossil sisters!'

'*Four hundred thousand?!*' whispered Marigold, Mabel and Morris. That number was bigger than any of them could really hold in their brains.

'As I said, some of these links may lead us down dead ends and some of them might be the jackpot, but we won't know until we start rummaging through them. How long have you got?'

Marigold looked up at the clock, as she was the best at telling the time. 'Lydia usually gives us an hour. We got here at four and now it's . . . quarter to five.'

'The library closes at five, I'm afraid!' Lady told them.

'We've only got fifteen minutes?' Morris said sulkily.

'That's plenty of time to find out a little bit about each sister. Shall we start with the youngest first?' Morris punched the air with both his fists, but didn't shout in case he got shushed by a nearby reader.

'Po-sy Fos-sil,' Lady spoke as she typed. She clicked on the first link and stood to let Morris sit down to get a closer look. There was a lot of writing, but Morris was focused on a photograph in the top right-hand corner of the screen.

'Can we click on that?' he asked, jabbing his finger at the glass.

'We can, but with the mouse.' Lady clicked the photograph for him, and it blew up to its full size. It was very grainy, but it was a colour photograph of Posy alone on a stage – her tights, leotard and tutu all pure, brilliant white. She stood on one leg on the very tip of her toes with the other perfectly straight leg lifted and stretched out behind her. She looked calm and even had a small smile on her lips. She was elegant and strong. Everything Morris aspired to be.

'Wow,' said Morris.

'Look at her!' Marigold squeezed her brother's shoulders, knowing just how special it was for him to see someone doing exactly what he would love to do one day.

'We've only got a few minutes left. You've seen a picture of Posy and I've told you all I know about Petrova, so I think it's only fair we quickly have a little look at what we can find on Pauline.' Lady gestured for Morris to stand and her long, slender fingers took to the keyboard once more.

'Can you also type in Pebble Theatre, as well as her name?' Marigold said quietly.

'Of course. Do you think she once performed there?'

'Maybe. I just . . . have a feeling.' Marigold looked sideways at her brother and sister who smiled back mischievously.

'It would appear your feeling was indeed correct. Look at this.' Lady clicked on 'Images' and lots of photographs popped up. Some were black-and-white, and others were like the photo of Posy – colour, but very grainy and faded. Lady clicked on the first photograph.

'That's the Pebble Theatre, isn't it?' Morris tapped the

screen again. 'Sorry,' he said, when he saw the greasy smudge he'd left behind. Lady polished it away with her handkerchief.

'It is indeed.' The theatre certainly hadn't changed much, if at all, over the years but Marigold was more interested in the faces of the three people standing in front of the theatre's front doors. Marigold didn't recognize the tallest woman, but she looked very glamorous. Her curly hair burst out of the back of a pink headscarf tied in a giant bow on the top of her head. It flopped over one of her eyes as she threw back her head and laughed at the child in her arms who was scowling at the camera. Next to the glamorous lady stood none other than Pauline Fossil, with a big grin on her bright red lips. She was wearing a white shirt with puffy sleeves and a black pencil skirt with small heels. She looked less wild than the other woman but still just as breathtakingly beautiful. The sign above their heads declared to the world that the show was Shakespeare's *Twelfth Night*, starring Pauline Fossil. It was all written in big bulbs that shone brightly, but something about the little girl kept drawing Marigold back to her little round face. At first glance Marigold didn't believe she knew her, but there was something about her eyes.

'Does it say who is in the photo?' she asked.

'Let's see.' Lady double-clicked the photograph and it disappeared for a moment, only to reappear much smaller on a website about London's theatres. 'There's an old newspaper article here. Let's see what it says. *Pauline Fossil . . .*' Lady read, '*pictured on the right, is to star in* Twelfth Night *at the Windmill Theatre.*'

'Is that what the Pebble Theatre was called before Bam took over?' asked Mabel.

'I suppose so.' Marigold shrugged.

'"*I couldn't be more pleased that Miss Fossil is joining us here at the Windmill,*" *says theatre owner and producer, Jean Cooper.*'

Morris's brow scrunched together. 'Cooper? Isn't that . . . ?'

'That's Bam's last name, isn't it?' Mabel asked.

'"*My daughter,*"' Lady continued, '"*is a big fan of Pauline's after we saw her appear in* Alice in Wonderland *when Maude was very little, so we hope Pauline will feel happy and at home here for the next few months.*"' Lady finished reading and she noticed quite quickly that the Pebbles had all gone very, very quiet.

'Maude?!' Morris gasped.

'So that photo is of Pauline Fossil . . .' said Mabel.

'Jean Cooper who owned the theatre . . .' said Lady.

'And our very own Brilliant Aunt Maude when she was a little girl,' said Marigold. 'So that must mean . . .'

'. . . that your Brilliant Aunt Maude actually knew Pauline Fossil,' finished Lady. Marigold, Mabel and Morris looked at each other with grins that stretched from ear to ear.

'There you are!' Lydia appeared from behind a bookshelf. She had an armful of books to read herself, mostly about money management and how to run a business. 'Hello, Lady. Have they been any trouble?'

'None at all,' Lady said as she shut down the computer.

'Did you find everything you wanted to find?' Lydia said, tucking her library card away.

'Yes.' Marigold nodded, and then she couldn't help but let a laugh of pure joy escape her. 'And then some!'

# 9

# The Jig Is Up

'Hi, Petunia!' the children chimed as they bobbed in single file through the cramped stage door.

'Hello, Mack!' Mabel said, bending down to greet the cat who meowed excitedly at the prospect of a bit of fuss. It was now nearly seven o'clock – they always dawdled home from the library, too engrossed in their newest finds. Morris seemed particularly impressed with his choice and had almost finished it by the time they were back at the theatre.

'Ahh, the great young minds return from the land of knowledge! Tell me, what great adventures did you bring home with you this time?' Petunia was what most people would call weird but to the children she was magnificent. Her black hair was always adorned with something dazzling. Once it was a golden headband covered in glittering stars, another time it was a tiny top hat with a silver spider sitting on its rim (which really freaked Morris out), but today it was a multicoloured patchwork flat cap. Petunia stayed behind her stage-door desk but poked her head through the hatch.

'I borrowed a book about Amelia Earhart!' said Mabel, signing herself in on the clipboard hung on the wall. Everyone who came in and out of the theatre had to sign themselves in and out. Petunia would need to know exactly who was in the theatre in case anything terrible happened, like a fire or if all the power went out. 'Did you know she was the first female pilot to fly solo across the Atlantic?' Mabel proudly showed the front cover of the book to Petunia. It was an illustration of Amelia Earhart with her hands on her hips looking upward as a plane flew past, trailing smoke in a perfectly straight line against a clear blue sky.

'Very good! Did *you* know that she mysteriously disappeared?' Petunia said, with a flourish of her hands as if she were a magician's assistant.

'Ahh, spoilers!' Mabel covered her ears with her book still in her hand.

'I got a couple of novels that were new in.' Marigold rearranged her rucksack on her shoulders, failing to mention that it contained one more book than she was letting on. 'I've read everything else.'

'And what about you, young Morris?' Petunia leant her chin in her hand, gazing at the children happily with a dopey smile. 'Anything to stimulate your imagination, hmm?'

'I borrowed a book all about the human body!' he said, turning another page and wincing at whatever it was he saw, scrunching up his nose in slight disgust,

'I didn't have you pegged as a biologist, my boy!'

'A dancer has to know what his body is doing and what it is capable of, in order to be the best he can be,' Morris said with a firm nod.

'You've got me there, old sport!' Petunia laughed, impressed. 'What's the face for, though?'

'I just think this book is telling me a bit more than I need to know!' Morris pretended to be sick and they all laughed at him.

'Well, thanks for a lovely outing, Lydia!' Marigold said with gusto. 'We're going to go upstairs and read our new books and –'

'Now wait just a minute, you three.' Lydia grabbed the hood of Marigold's coat before she had a chance to dash through the door and disappear into the many nooks and crannies of the theatre. She might not find them again for hours if she let them go now. 'You've all got some explaining to do.'

'A-about what, Lydia?' Marigold tried to smile, but she was very hot all of a sudden and she could feel a bead of sweat beginning to trickle down her forehead.

'*You* tell *me*! What's with all the whispering? The skulking around the bookshelves and . . . and the googling!'

'Googling?' Petunia raised an eyebrow.

'What was so important that you needed Lady's help today?' Lydia folded her arms across her chest.

'We're writing essays for s-school . . .' Marigold stuttered.

'Why can't we just tell her?' Mabel whispered out of the corner of her mouth.

'We promised we wouldn't!' hissed Morris.

'Maybe if we told her,' Mabel continued, 'Lydia could help.'

'*Children* . . .' Lydia warned. Marigold looked up at her. *She looks so worried*, Marigold thought. The circles under her eyes were definitely darker than they used to be. Finally, Marigold took a deep breath and said, 'Please don't be angry with us.'

# 10

## Bam Returns

Up in the kitchen at the top of the theatre, Marigold set down the journal in front of Lydia.

'This?' Lydia's face went bright red and her eyes began to tear up. 'This is what all the fuss has been about? A book? This is why you've been so secretive?' The Pebbles nodded, none of them quite able to muster the right words. 'Kids . . .' Lydia sighed the biggest sigh the Pebbles had ever heard (and they'd heard her sigh quite a lot). 'You three scared the life out of me. I thought someone was upset or in trouble or danger!' She put her head in her hands and laughed.

'Sorry, Lydia,' the children mumbled.

'We really didn't mean to worry you.' Morris ran to put his arms round her shoulders.

'It was Marigold that made us keep it a secret.' Mabel elbowed her sister gently in the ribs.

'Thanks, Mabel,' Marigold mumbled. 'I just thought we could work out who it belonged to on our own.'

'Like your own little adventure?' Lydia asked, and Marigold lowered her eyes, feeling a little foolish. 'I understand.' Lydia smiled her kindest smile. 'Come on, then. What is it? Tell me all about it.' The Pebbles launched into the story of how Marigold found the journal and how excited they all were to be reading about the actress, the pilot and the dancer. They all talked over each other and Lydia couldn't help but laugh.

'Well, Pebbles,' she finally said, turning the journal over in her hands, 'you've certainly stumbled across something quite miraculous.'

'Do you really think so, Lydia?' Marigold sat down next to her.

'I *know* so.' Lydia smiled, stroking Marigold's sleek hair.

'How?' Morris asked.

'Not a lot of people make it into the history books, even when they make history. The Fossil sisters may not be known globally for their achievements but there is someone who remembers the Fossils. Someone who will be very interested in seeing this journal.'

'Who?' the Pebbles asked, leaning in to listen to Lydia's voice, which had now become quite quiet and mysterious.

'Someone who was acquainted with the Fossil sisters personally. Someone who actually knew one of them. Someone who would be beside themselves to read this journal and relive their adventures.'

'Bam?' asked Marigold.

'But she's been gone for ages! When is she coming home?' added Morris.

'Now . . .' said a voice behind them. The three Pebbles slowly turned to the doorway and there stood none other than Brilliant Aunt Maude.

# 11

# Listening at the Door

'Bam!' The children all leapt at the woman in the doorway, and she dropped her bags in order to wrap her arms round them. Morris rushed in first and almost got lost in the many layers of her oversized black faux-fur coat. She must have been awfully hot, but she'd always said that suffering the heat was worth how spectacular it made her feel.

'My beautiful little Pebbles! How I've missed you!' Bam suddenly pulled away and gave them each in turn a very stern look indeed. 'You've grown. The lot of you. You've all grown up! So much! How dare you? I told you not to grow at all, not even an inch, until I got home.' The children would have laughed had she not looked so deadly serious. 'I haven't come empty-handed! Hold out your hands and close your eyes.' The Pebbles did as they were told, but Morris found the suspense too much and couldn't stop giggling. 'Open!' The children looked down into their cupped hands, where there sat, for each of them, a brand-new pebble.

'Marigold, I found yours in Peru.' It was small and jet black, flat and smooth. Without thinking, Marigold held its cold surface to her cheek and felt calmed. 'Mabel, yours is from Italy.' Mabel's was a faded pink colour and had a hole right through the middle. She held it up to her eye and looked at her aunt through it. 'I thought maybe you could put a piece of string through it and make a nice necklace.'

'What about mine, Bam? Where's mine from?' Morris bounced.

'Well, dear Morris, your pebble is not actually a pebble at all. It's sea glass!'

'Sea glass?' Morris held it up to the light and realized it was a little transparent.

'Glass that's made its way into the sea and been moulded and shaped by the movement of the waves to create a beautiful stone. It's come all the way from Hawaii!' The children turned the stones over in their hands and marvelled at just how far they had come to be with them. While they looked at their pebbles, Bam marvelled at her own.

'I blame you for this.' She stood up and hugged a smiling

Lydia so tight that Lydia stopped smiling and mouthed '*Ouch!*' at the children over Bam's shoulders.

'For what?' Lydia laughed.

'How much they've grown up.'

When Bam finally let go, Lydia said, 'All children grow up, Bam.'

'Whatever for?' Bam trilled as she walked over to the kitchen sink, took a colander from the drying rack and popped it on top of her grey curls. 'I didn't!' The Pebbles fell about laughing.

'Oh, Bam, you never change.' Lydia sighed with a smile, shaking her head.

'Exactly! None of you should either.'

'We're so pleased you came back for our summer holiday!' Marigold grinned.

'Technically, you're a few days late though. We only have five and a half weeks left!' moaned Mabel.

'Five and a half weeks is an awfully long time, Mabel.' Lydia laughed.

'I wouldn't have been late had I not heard whispers of a snake charmer in Egypt, but he got a rather nasty bite from his cobra before I could get to him.' Bam shrugged, as if that was the most normal thing she could have said. 'Now what's all this about Pauline, Petrova and Posy? I've not heard those names in years and, as soon as I walk through my own theatre doors, it's all you can talk about!' The children went terribly quiet. Lydia gave Marigold an encouraging look and slid the journal across the table to her.

'I found this. Hidden in the wall.' Marigold walked over to Bam and placed the journal in her hands. There was a satisfying tappity-tap as her long red nails touched the hard cover. Bam didn't look at it for very long before she began to smile.

'Did you find it in dressing room nine?'

'Yes.' Marigold nodded.

'Behind the wall?' Her smile became wider.

'How did you . . . ?'

'I helped Pauline make the hole!' Bam said, as if she were having a flashback. And she guffawed loud enough to wake up the entire street. 'Goodness! It's funny what you forget when you've lived as many years as I have. I'm three hundred and six, don't you know?' She winked at Morris, whose mouth fell open.

'She's only joking,' Mabel whispered, which was met with a frown from Bam.

'Prove it,' Bam whispered back to Mabel, and when Mabel's mouth began to open and close, flapping like a fish, Bam continued. 'That's right, we used the key to her door to poke through the plaster and then a teaspoon to scoop it all away in bigger chunks.'

'We saw a picture of you when you were a little girl with your mum – Jean Cooper – and Pauline outside the theatre.'

'Yes, it was the Windmill back then. When I took over, I renamed it. I'd filled the place with so many seaside pebbles it couldn't possibly remain the Windmill now, could it?'

'What happened to Pauline?'

'We used to write to each other. Back and forth and back and forth but then . . . well . . . life got in the way! She always said she'd love to come back here but actors only ever go where there's work.' Bam shrugged her shoulders up to her ears and let them fall back down with a great big sigh. 'No show ever brought her our way again.'

'Surely she'd be welcome back now, wouldn't she?' Lydia asked.

'Of *course* she would! Once you've come to the Pebble Theatre, you're part of the family for life! Goodness knows we could use something new to draw in the crowds.' Marigold caught Lydia shaking her head quickly but fiercely at Brilliant Aunt Maude and, when Lydia saw her looking, she quickly transformed her frown into a smile – but it didn't quite reach her eyes. 'She'd be welcome back any time,' Bam said, forcing a similar smile.

'Bam, is she still . . . well . . . you know . . .' Marigold began cautiously.

'Spit it out, girl, it's getting late and I'm ready for my glorious bed,' Bam said.

'. . . *alive*.' Marigold whispered. Bam chuckled.

'You are a morbid little thing. Truth be told, I'm not

certain. If I'm three hundred and seven and we met when I was a little girl, she'd be nearing about three hundred and fifty by now.' Lydia shook her head with a smile at her mad but Brilliant Aunt Maude.

'You said you were three hundred and six,' said a voice from behind Mabel's hair.

'That's because I've aged a year already since being home. I forgot what hard work you three are. You ask so many questions, my brain has turned to porridge. If I sleep with a bowl under my head, I'll have enough breakfast for us all tomorrow.'

'Yes, I think that's enough excitement for one evening. We'll pick this up tomorrow, children.' Lydia began to herd them towards the door.

'Uhhhhhh!' they all groaned at the unfairness of being kept in such suspense.

'I thought you'd be excited to head to bed considering you've got such good bedtime reading material.'

'That's true! Mabel's reading tonight but I can't wait until it's my turn.' Morris puffed out his chest.

'Your turn?' Bam asked.

'I'm Posy!' Morris said, as he did a perfect pirouette in his socks on the kitchen floor.

'Wonderful, Morris!' Bam gave him a little round of applause, but Morris's brow furrowed.

'You don't seem surprised, Bam. I'm very good at dancing now. I think it's what I want to do when I'm older.'

'To be honest, I'm *not* very surprised, Morris. You came to me in a shoebox, so it comes as no shock that your feet are destined for greatness!'

'I'm reading Petrova's journal entries!' Mabel shoved her brother out of the way, held out her arms, flew like an aeroplane round the kitchen table and planted a kiss on Bam's cheek.

'And I'm Pauline.' Marigold picked up the journal and clutched it with both arms across her chest.

'I can see the Fossils have made quite the impression on the three of you.'

'I'm still not sure . . .' Mabel said, biting her lip.

'Of what?' Bam asked.

'Well, they wanted to be super, mega famous.'

'They wanted to get their names in the history books,' Marigold corrected.

'But they didn't manage it. So how good could they have really been at acting, flying and dancing if no one took any notice?'

'You're taking notice now, aren't you? It doesn't always matter if you become famous or not. Sometimes, it's enough just to make a difference to those around you. For your story, no matter how grand or small, to live on and continue being told after you're gone. The fact you're talking about them all these years later is a job well done, I'd say,' Bam said, and Mabel smiled.

'Come on now, you three,' said Lydia. 'Up to bed. I'll be there in a moment. Your Brilliant Aunt and I need to have a little catch-up.'

The Pebbles scooted out of the room, excited to carry on reading, but Bam's words had been tinged with a sadness that none of them could quite understand. As soon as the kitchen door closed, they turned to each other.

'Oh, I'm so pleased Bam is home at last,' Morris said, grinning.

'Me too, but don't you think she seemed sort of . . . sad?' replied Mabel.

'Yes, I picked up on that too,' added Marigold. 'Maybe she's just tired. She's probably come from a long, long way away.'

'That's true.'

It was then that they heard Lydia's voice rise a little on the other side of the door.

'Are they arguing?' Morris's eyes widened. He'd never heard Lydia get properly cross before.

'I don't think so, but just to be sure . . .' Mabel slowly opened the door a tiny bit so they could hear a little better.

'Don't Mabel! It's rude to eavesdrop!' Marigold whispered, but didn't move to stop her sister.

'I'm not eavesdropping; I'm just . . . concerned that the people I love are angry with each other and I'm . . . I'm . . . trying to help.' Marigold rolled her eyes, but she couldn't help leaning in to hear better.

'Lydia, there's nothing more I can do. The Pebble Theatre is old. Outdated. On the way out,' Bam said quietly.

'On the way out?' Morris mouthed at his sisters.

'Surely there are plenty of performers out there.' Marigold could see Lydia sit down opposite Bam, her back to them.

'There are. Of *course* there are. Before I left, I knew exactly where I was going and I had a list of performers I was interested in. I was going to bring them all back here to restore a bit of excitement and . . . well . . . money! But none of them wanted to travel away from their homes, and I can't offer them enough money to tempt them here. We have to face facts, Lydia. I can't afford to keep this theatre running any more. We aren't selling enough tickets.'

'What about everyone who works here? The front-of-house staff, box office, crew, cleaners, the cast . . . ?'

'It's a miracle I've been able to pay everyone's wages this long,' Bam admitted, not quite able to meet Lydia's eye. 'Don't worry, I'll make sure everyone finds somewhere new to go before the doors close.'

'I have no doubt you'll see everyone safely off Ship Pebble but . . . what does that mean for us? For the children? We *live* here.' The children could hear a sob rise in Lydia's throat. None of them could bear to look at each other, for fear of crying themselves.

'We'll all be fine. I'll sell the theatre to the highest bidder and we'll do well enough from it to buy a little house somewhere quiet. I can live out the rest of my days reading plays I'll never produce. Maybe I'll even write one. And the children will grow up to be whatever they want to be.'

'You'd never be happy sitting still reading plays for the rest of your life, Bam, and you know it.'

'Maybe not, but right now I don't have much of a choice.'

'And what about me?'

'You'll be fine.'

'This theatre is my life. Those children are my life.'

'And they still will be! But you would also be free to do whatever your heart has always desired. I know this theatre isn't your idea of an ideal life. You stayed because of me and those gorgeous children. But this would set you free. You could go back to school, if you wanted. Work in a theatre that actually makes money!' Bam laughed, but it caught in her throat. 'You are so bright and so marvellous. It wouldn't be fair of us to drag you away from the life you could have.'

Lydia stayed quiet and the children wondered exactly what life Lydia wanted that she'd never been able to have. They'd never thought of her as anything other than the woman who looked after them, and would look after them until they left. They suddenly felt very selfish.

'The life I want is the life I have, Bam. Sure, I'll admit that those three little gremlins came along and completely turned our lives upside down but . . . well . . . would you have it any other way?' There was another silence and Marigold couldn't help but look through the crack in the door. Lydia and Bam were staring at each other, searching each other's eyes for answers. Finally, Bam broke her gaze and shook her head, her lips curving into a small smile.

'No. No, I suppose I wouldn't.'

'*Exactly*.' Lydia reached out and took Bam's hand, careful not to get scratched on any of her long red talons. 'We're a family, Bam. We might be a little lopsided, a bit mismatched and frayed around the edges, but we're a family nonetheless. And families stick together, no matter what. Even when your feet are tired, the sky is dark and you've got nothing left to say. Families pull each other close and carry on. Together.' Lydia's cheeks flushed pink and she seemed a little out of breath, but she finished with a firm nod like a full stop to her speech.

'OK.' Bam nodded. 'How do we tell the children that we have to sell the theatre?' Morris, Mabel and Marigold all exchanged sheepish, guilty looks.

'Gently, and in the right way – but not just yet. Let's give them at least one more week of blissful theatre summer fun.'

# 12

## Petrova

'I just can't believe it! I just . . . can't.' Morris opened the door to the bedroom, leapt on to his bed in one giant bound and began to bounce softly with nervous energy.

'I know,' said Marigold, sitting cross-legged at the end of her own bed and shaking her head. 'I can't believe we have to sell the theatre.'

'No, not that!' Morris said, beginning to bounce higher. 'I can't believe that Bam is giving up! That's not like her at all! Usually she's all fired up in the face of adversity. She'd usually be all like . . . "OVER MY DEAD BODY!" and "NOT IF I HAVE ANYTHING TO DO WITH IT" or "I'LL GIVE

THEM WHAT FOR!". That's not Brilliant Aunt Maude downstairs. That's . . . that's *Boring* Aunt Maude.' He galumphed down on to his bed, making the floorboards creak beneath.

'Keep the noise down or they'll hear you,' Marigold hushed.

'I don't care if they hear me. They're the ones keeping stupid secrets.'

'He's right. These are secrets that affect all of us, not just them. They should have told us straight away,' Mabel said, as Mack pushed open their door with his head and jumped on to her lap.

'I know.' Marigold bit her lip. 'But . . . they're doing what they think is best for us.' She shrugged. Morris rolled his eyes and Mabel crossed her arms over her chest. Both were unconvinced. 'If you want to tell them we were listening at the door, be my guest.' They both fidgeted a little. 'We had our secret,' Marigold held up the journal. 'Let's let them have theirs, for a while at least.' Mabel and Morris visibly deflated a little, which was a sure sign they were giving in. Marigold decided a distraction would be best.

'Lydia talked an awful lot about "family", didn't she?' Morris picked up a pillow from his bed and hugged it to himself, hiding his face a little from view.

'I suppose so,' Marigold replied. Morris didn't look at his sister — he knew that if he did, he wouldn't be able to ask what he was about to.

'Do you ever . . . think about them?' he ventured.

94

'Who? Lydia and Bam?' Mabel asked.

'No! I mean . . . your *real* families?' There was a heavy silence that filled the air between them.

'Sometimes, yeah,' Mabel said quietly.

'Me too.' Marigold nodded. 'I think it'd be a bit weird if we didn't.' Morris hugged his pillow tighter and lifted it slightly so neither of his sisters could see his face at all.

'It's your turn, Mabel,' Marigold said as brightly as she could and handed over the journal with a dramatic flourish, as if The Passing of the Journal were a sacred ceremony.

'All right, Shakespeare. Calm down,' Mabel said, and was relieved to hear Morris chuckle from behind his barrier. 'We're only reading someone's old diary. It's hardly a great work of literature.' Mabel took the book fiercely and rifled through the pages with a carelessness that made Marigold wince.

'Maybe you could turn the journal into a book, Marigold? A proper one!' Morris chimed.

'*Ha, ha.*' Marigold rolled her eyes instinctively.

'I . . . I was being serious,' replied Morris, and Marigold could feel that she'd bitten back a little hard at Morris's kindness so she put a hand on his shoulder and said, 'Sorry. Thank you. But I don't think I'm quite there yet.'

Together they assembled their little reading den on Marigold's bed, with the quilt tossed over their heads and the glittering fairy lights tossed into the centre of their circle.

'Can I start reading yet or not?'

Marigold and Morris shuffled their bums on the bed to get comfy.

'OK,' Morris declared. 'We're ready.'

*25 October 1939*

*Dear Pauline and Posy,*

*Life with Gum is boring.*

'Why do I get the boring bit?' Mabel whined.

'Who's Gum?' asked Morris.

'Keep going! I bet it gets interesting!' Marigold urged.

*He's the same as usual. The grumbling has just got worse as he gets older. However, now that I've been promoted to studying aeroplane engines, I'm spending a lot more time at the aerodrome. It's so close to the house and couldn't feel more like home. Nobby is wonderful, too. He has taught me everything there is to know about being a mechanic.*

'Nobby?' Mabel scrunched up her nose.

'That's the man Lady said she couldn't remember! He helped her repair Spitfires!' said Morris.

'Wow!' Mabel's eyes began to sparkle.

*I reckon I could fix up a plane better than he could, although he'd rather hate to admit it. A girl being better* at his own job than him? Never! He's quite brilliant, though. I do think I like him rather a lot. He takes me flying all the time and it's so utterly marvellous, Fossils. It really is! Far better than I ever could have imagined. Problems always look so much smaller from above the clouds, and if a day is getting a little hard it only takes a quick spin around the sky to make me feel all right again. You'll have to come and visit when I can fly by myself. Then I shall be able to take you on a flight! One by one, mind, but still! Don't tell Nana or Garnie, though. They'd never let us go flying together in a million years.

I'm hoping to get my pilot's licence in time to help with this blasted war that's broken out. I hate the war, but I've started to wonder if maybe there's something I can do to help those affected by it. I don't really want to get involved in all the nasty business but if I'm able to help it stop sooner, that's a different matter.

Twinkletoes, you're next. I want to read everything there is to know about Czechoslovakia. What is the food like? Are the people nice? How often are you dancing? Pauline, next time you get the diary I want to read more embarrassing stories. Your lives are much more glamorous than mine, so I need evidence that you've not changed. I hope the fame and attention haven't gone to your heads and that you didn't forget

*your poor, plain and boring sister as soon as you set
foot on foreign soil*

*Quite frankly, I'm utterly appalled you didn't include
a photograph of some kind, Pauline, so I'll start. I took
this on Gum's camera. He never uses it so I doubt he'll
notice, but, even so, you're sworn to secrecy.*

*Love to you both!*

*Your high-flying sister,
Petrova*

Mabel stayed staring at the journal for a moment. Marigold
gave her a nudge. 'Let us see too, silly!'

Mabel jolted out of her daze and turned the book round as
if she were a teacher reading a story to a class and showing
off the illustrations, but this was no illustration. This was a
black-and-white photograph of Petrova Fossil herself, stuck
into the book. She had dark hair that stuck out under the
strap of her flying goggles. She was grinning, with her hands
on her hips, and behind her was a silver aeroplane with
propellers that were glinting in the sun.

'Wow. What a girl!' they said.

# 13

# The Woman in Pink

The following morning felt strange to the Pebble children. Marigold awoke with a frown, but was unsure what particular worry had caused her face to crease in such a way. She usually woke hungry, but today the empty feeling was in her heart and not her tummy. It was only when she looked up from her bed in her sleepy state that she saw her brother and sister were also sitting up in their beds with similarly puzzled expressions.

'I feel . . . weird,' said Marigold.

'Me too,' said Mabel.

'Me three,' said Morris.

'Meow,' said Mack from the bottom of Mabel's bed. The

news of losing the theatre was certainly weighing them down.

'Can you hear voices?' Mabel asked. Marigold and Morris listened and suddenly a familiar voice yelled out, 'Don't you dare speak to me in that tone!' Mabel swiftly turned towards the window behind her bed and drew back the curtains. Her window was directly above the front of the theatre and they often liked to crowd around and watch the audience come in for the nightly show. They hadn't done that in a long while, as now the audiences only consisted of a very few people who were often returning customers they'd seen a million times before. This time, however, the children were the audience for a show they didn't expect to see.

'Oh, no. It's Bam! And she looks pretty angry,' Mabel said, and Marigold and Morris came rushing over to get a good look. Bam was outside, holding a giant placard that said FOR SALE in big red writing – and she had a bright red face to match. She was waving the sign about haphazardly, and it was getting dangerously close to the face of a woman the Pebble children had never seen before.

'That's a very, *very* nice outfit,' said Mabel. Marigold and Morris both nodded their agreement. The woman wore a pencil skirt, a smart double-breasted jacket, a hat with a big floppy brim and high heels – all entirely in baby pink.

'I wonder who she is,' said Morris, his face so close to the window that the glass had begun to fog.

'Does that sign say FOR SALE?' asked Marigold.

'Is that woman going to buy our theatre?!' whimpered Mabel.

'Well, we can't get any of those questions answered up here. Shall we go outside and find out?' Marigold suggested, and they all scurried off the bed in a blur of pyjamas.

'I'm going to go and wake Lydia,' Marigold said, as she jammed her feet into her fluffy slippers and tied her purple dressing gown round herself. 'Bam looks ever so cross. She looked like she was going to knock that woman out! Lydia will know just what to say to calm her down and fix the situation.'

Lydia might have been even more cross at Bam than Bam was at the mystery woman in pink. She strode outside in bare feet, seeming not to feel the cold of the paving slabs against her soles.

'What on *earth* do you think you're doing?!' she yelled, tearing the sign out of Bam's hands. The Pebble children didn't dare get any closer than they had to, so they stayed in the doorway of the main entrance of the theatre. Everyone's voices were raised anyway, so they could hear the conversation very clearly.

'What am *I* doing?! What is *she* doing?!' The woman said nothing, but stuck her nose in the air – her large pink-rimmed sunglasses shielding most of her face from view. Her lips were glossy and plump, pinned together quite tightly, and her eyebrows rose above the frames of her glasses in perfect arches.

'I'm sorry,' Lydia said, trying a calmer tone and a forced smile. 'But who are you exactly?' The woman finally lowered her gaze and looked Lydia up and down then back up again.

'I'm Trixabellina von Hustle . . .' She dropped her sunglasses down to the very tip of her upturned nose to reveal eyes that were an entrancing shade of green and added, 'the Third. And I'm here to buy your theatre.' Her accent definitely wasn't British.

'Where's she from?' whispered Mabel.

'She talks like all the people in the movies I watch. *Singin' in the Rain*, *Anchors Aweigh*, *On the Town*. She's definitely American,' Morris said, with the hint of a proud smile.

'You seem to be mistaken,' Lydia said as kindly as she could, given the circumstances, but still with a clipped tone. 'The theatre is *not* for sale.'

'Your maid's sign begs to differ.' The woman in pink's face didn't seem to move even a millimetre when she spoke. There was not one line or wrinkle in her face whatsoever.

'*Maid?!* Did she just say *maid*?!' screeched Bam. 'Lydia, give me that sign back because I'm about to shove it right up her —'

'Does she always talk like this when there are children present?' asked Trixabellina. Lydia spun round and saw Marigold, Mabel and Morris all crammed in the doorway and, despite their slightly guilty, yet reassuring, smiles, she put her face in her hands and groaned.

'Bam, please, just . . . don't say anything else. We promised not to tell the children just yet, and you waving that sign around does not help!' Lydia whispered while rubbing her temples. 'This is my aunt Maude. She owns the theatre.'

'Mmm, she's very professional.' Trixabellina pointed her nose back towards the sky.

'And I am her niece, Lydia.'

'And what do *you* do?' Trixabellina said, jabbing a pink-painted manicured nail at Lydia's head.

'I'm . . . I'm the stage manager here.'

'Well, don't expect to be kept on when everything changes hands.'

'There'll be no change of hands while I'm still alive!' Bam rolled up her sleeves and Lydia quickly held out a protective arm.

'I'm sorry,' Lydia forced a smile that twitched at the corners. 'There seems to be some kind of mistake.' Trixabellina didn't bother trying to smile at all. She meant business.

'A mistake?' An eyebrow was raised above Trixabellina's sunglasses.

'Yes, we've not quite ironed out all of the details yet. That sign certainly shouldn't have gone up just yet.' Lydia adjusted her position to hide the big letters from the children's view.

'It'll be that estate agent I spoke to about putting the theatre on the market,' Bam grumbled quietly, so the children couldn't hear. 'He's only gone and jumped the bloomin' gun.'

'So, the theatre isn't for sale?'

'No, it is. Well, it will be,' Lydia admitted in a whisper, praying the children couldn't hear her. 'But can I ask what you want a theatre for? Are you a producer?'

'Oh, goodness me, no! I couldn't give two flying monkeys about *theatre*.' She spat the word as if it left a nasty taste in her mouth. 'No, I've wanted a little dream house in London for a while. This would make a perfect mansion. All those gross dressing rooms could be turned into luxurious bedrooms, and the auditorium? Just imagine the size of that living room!' Trixabellina clapped her hands together in glee. Lydia's face had gradually turned twice as pink as Trixabellina's jacket. The children thought she might pop with anger.

'Well, in that case the theatre *is* for sale . . . just not to *you*.' There was a long pause in which Trixabellina simply stared through her dark glasses at Lydia. The three Pebbles held their breath, straining to hear and completely unsure what was going to happen next. Was another fight going to break out? Would they all need to rush in and hold Brilliant Aunt Maude back as they went at each other tooth and nail? They'd never seen Bam truly angry, but the taste they'd had of her being a little bit annoyed was enough to make sure they were always well behaved in her presence.

Finally, Trixabellina sniffed and said, 'Hmm. You'll be seeing me a lot sooner than you think.' She turned on her pink heels and floated down the steps of the theatre into a waiting white limousine. The family watched as her car glided down the road.

# 14

## Hope for Breakfast

In the afternoon that followed the visit from the woman in pink, Marigold learnt she was not good at keeping secrets – a trait it seemed she had got from Lydia. Lydia found it excruciatingly difficult to keep the secret that the theatre would have to be sold. Especially after Bam's outburst that morning. It weighed heavily on her heart, and every time she opened her mouth she ran the risk that it would come spilling out. Marigold, however, was struggling with the secret that she already *knew* Lydia's secret. They tiptoed around each other and avoided conversations longer than a 'Hello' and 'What's for dinner?'. Mabel and Morris found it much easier to occupy themselves and their brains. Reading a good book or playing a fun game seemed to do just the trick, but Marigold was really struggling. It felt like an alien was in her stomach, growing bigger and bigger because it was eating her from the inside out until, the following morning, she exploded at the kitchen table during breakfast.

'*We know!*' she yelled. Lydia jumped so hard she spilt her orange juice, Morris bit his lip instead of his toast and marmalade, Mabel missed her mouth and dropped her cereal on her lap, Mack jumped off the table, hissing furiously, and Bam threw her newspaper into the air, the pages floating down around them all in the silence.

'Kn-know what, d-darling?' Lydia asked, fetching a tea towel to mop up her spilt juice and throwing another to Mabel, who was wiping warm oats off her pyjamas with a scowl.

'Marigold! Thtop it!' Morris lisped, clutching his slightly swollen lip.

'*WE KNOW ABOUT THE THEATRE!*' Marigold had completely lost control.

'*Marigold!*' Mabel yelled, but she had to admit that as soon as the words had come tumbling from Marigold's lips she felt a weight lift off her shoulders.

'*WE KNOW YOU HAVE TO SELL IT!*' Marigold cried, then clasped both hands over her mouth to avoid anything else escaping.

'Oh dear,' Lydia said. 'How did you figure it out?' Marigold shook her head – her mouth still covered, her eyes wide – not able to trust herself with saying anything more just yet in case she yelled it.

'I think it was the giant FOR SALE sign Bam was waving outside the theatre yesterday that gave it away . . .' Mabel said.

'Maude . . .' Lydia groaned.

'We would have had to tell them eventually, Lydia. It's best they know.' Bam laughed, pouring herself another cup of steaming coffee from the pot. Lydia took a deep breath and composed herself.

'Also, we may have overheard you talking the night Bam came home,' admitted Marigold.

'You mean you were eavesdropping,' Bam corrected.

'No! Well . . . maybe. But thurely now we know, we can help!' said Morris, jumping to his feet.

'I don't think there's much to be done.' Lydia put her elbows on the table and slumped her head into her hands.

'Of courth there ith. There hath to be!' he pleaded.

'Nmm-imm-pomm-bmm,' mumbled Marigold behind her fingers. They all looked at her, their eyebrows raised. She dropped her hands and said, 'Nothing's impossible. Even the word impossible says "I'm possible". Audrey Hepburn said that.'

'Well, Audrey Hepburn never had to worry about keeping

a theatre open, and running, and four children safe,' replied Lydia.

'Three . . .' said Marigold, counting their heads.

'Four,' Lydia corrected, pointing at Bam, who rolled her eyes at her niece.

'What would it take? To thhhhave the thhheatre?' asked Morris.

'Oh, I don't know.' Bam threw up her hands and huffed. 'It would take enough tickets being sold to make enough money to guarantee that the theatre had a future. Ideally a future of selling even more tickets and making even more money.'

'And what would we have to do to do that?' The cogs in Mabel's head had begun turning.

'Put on a show.'

'We have a show on every night!' Marigold chirped. *Problem solved!* she thought.

'Not just any show, my love. It would have to be *the* show. The most spectacular show London has ever seen. A show so brilliant that no one feels they could possibly miss out on seeing it. A show so marvellous people would want to come back to see it again and again.'

'I wish it were simpler, kids. I really do.' Lydia shrugged.

'That sounds pretty simple to me.' Mabel mimicked Lydia's shrug.

'Simple? *Mabel*. We'd have to find a show to put on, hire a cast, promote the show so well that it sells out, rehearse and then put it on,' Bam retorted.

Mabel counted quietly on her fingers. 'That's just five things, *Maude*.'

Morris stifled a laugh and even Marigold couldn't help but smile. Bam scowled.

'Isn't it at least worth a try, Bam?' Marigold asked cautiously. 'As long as we're together I'm sure we'll be fine, no matter where we end up . . . but Pebble Theatre is where Pebbles *really* belong.'

'All Pebbles in favour of trying their hardest to save the theatre, say "aye" . . .' Morris said as he put his hand out, palm down over the table.

'AYE!' Mabel shouted and slammed her hand down on top of Morris's.

'Ouch!' He winced.

'Sorry. Excited,' she spat, with a mouth still full of cereal. Marigold gently placed her hand over her sister's.

'Sorry, Bam. I know this makes things a little more complicated for you. Trying to save the theatre is much harder than just letting it go, but sometimes the right thing isn't always the easiest thing.'

'And who said that?' Bam smirked.

'Me, I guess.' Marigold shrugged and Bam smiled at her fondly.

'Don't be sorry, Marigold,' Lydia said, and put her own

hand over Marigold's. 'You're right. This is our home and we shouldn't give it up without a fight. Bam, what say you?'

Brilliant Aunt Maude stood with much more vim and vigour than the rest of them thought she had for someone who claimed to be three hundred and six. 'For a moment there I almost lost my fire. How could I possibly think of giving up when there's so much to fight for? Especially with that awful fluorescent ninny sniffing around, who almost jumped in my grave while it was still warm! Ghastly woman. Awful, awful lady. Who has a name like Thumbelina anyway?' Bam scoffed, and the children giggled.

'You can hardly talk when your name is half of a Flintstones character!' Lydia snorted.

'We have to save our theatre from the likes of *Tinkerbell von Brussel Sprout the Third*.' Lydia expertly mimicked her accent, straightened her back and stuck her nose up just like Trixabellina. The Pebbles laughed, and even Bam couldn't help smirking through her distaste for the woman in pink.

'I'm *in*.' Bam put both her hands round the cluster of hands and wrapped her family's fingers in her red talons. 'Let's save our lovely theatre,' Bam said to Marigold, and gave her a smile that instantly made Marigold feel much better. She felt something rise up from the pit of her stomach, like a light growing bigger and bigger and brighter and brighter until it shone out of her face in a grin wider than she'd ever grinned before. A feeling that radiated out of her and reached Mabel,

Morris, Lydia and Bam, so that they all began smiling too. A feeling so strong, it made them all feel like anything was possible and that feeling was *hope*.

'We need a plan,' said Marigold.

Bam rubbed her hands together and said, 'What we need is a *show*.'

# 15

## Morris's Idea

Bam decided it was time to let the rest of the Pebble Theatre family in on their plans.

'Families don't keep secrets,' she said. 'Unless that secret is where the Christmas presents are hidden.' She rallied the troops into the auditorium and explained that the theatre was in danger.

'The simple truth of the matter, which I'm sure will come as no shock to you all, is that there is no money coming in,' Bam said, throwing up her hands, at which Theodore promptly burst into tears. 'All is not lost, dear Theo. We have a plan. If we can find a new and exciting show to put on very quickly to bring people in, we might just be able to save the theatre before we go under.'

'We're in, Bam,' Dante said, and Dawson gave one solitary slow nod.

'Whatever you need!' the Fortune Sisters chirped.

'You know you can count on us,' said Cora.

'What she said,' added Layton.

'The future's always changing,' said Petunia. She was wearing a headband that had lots of tiny stars on springs that shook and sparkled as she moved her head. 'Nothing's set in stone.'

'Theo, I'll take your crying as a "Yes, I can help"?' said Bam. Theo nodded and gave one more great heaving sob. 'Then let's get to work!'

The theatre had plenty of scripts and scores from shows gone by. There were dozens of each piled from floor to ceiling, but Bam was on a rampage.

'Not these, we've done these shows far too many times.' Bam lifted a large, heavy pile with ease and passed them to Lydia, who almost collapsed under the weight.

'What are you looking for?' Marigold asked as Bam fished a still-snoring Mack out of a box. The cat, startled out of his sleep, leapt from Marigold's arms and into Mabel's.

'Something. Anything. I need inspiration and these just won't do!' She knocked over a pile of copies of *Sweeney Todd*, some of which still had fake blood splatters over their clean white fronts. Morris leapt back as they fell at his feet and stared at them with wide eyes.

'How about a nice happy show? A comedy? With lots of dancing?' said Morris, giving his feet a little shuffle-hop-step.

'How about *A Little Princess*?' suggested Marigold.

'Or *Annie*!' said Mabel.

'Or how about a ballet?' shouted Morris.

'I don't think you'll get many of us dancing well enough, I'm afraid,' Theo said, pointing to his thick-soled black boots.

'No, no, no. It *has* to be something new. Something exciting.' Bam tapped her long nails on pile after pile, scanning title after title. None of them took her fancy.

'Nothing says exciting quite like pyros and stunts! Lots of sword fights and explosions!' said Theo, his eyes lighting up.

'I think we need to keep it as simple and . . . cheap as possible,' Bam said.

'Besides, I'd say magic and illusions are far more exciting than explosions!' said Dante, deftly fanning out a pack of cards with one hand.

'Magic tricks always take up too much rehearsal time.' Bam shooed Dante out of the way to get to more boxes behind him.

'*Oklahoma*?' Cora tried.

'Too old.'

'*My Fair Lady*?' Layton bravely attempted.

'Ancient.'

'*Oliver!?*' Petunia whispered meekly.

'Practically prehistoric! This is useless! We'll never find something that's *just right*.' Bam went to the window, and stared forlornly down to the street below. No one so much as glanced at her beautiful theatre as they marched past on their busy ways. Lydia went to her and gently put a hand on Bam's shoulder.

'Surely it has to be something everyone will know, or no one will want to come and watch. That would completely defeat the point.' When Bam didn't respond, Lydia began quickly rifling through more of the boxes, trying to find suggestions closer to Bam's seemingly impossible standards before she completely lost all faith. She gestured to the gang to do the same, hoping that their forthright attitude might spur Bam on to be a little more positive.

'Yes, I suppose you're right, dear niece. But, then again, it can't be something everyone has seen a million times before or no one will find the fun in coming to see it again this time.' If Bam wasn't being as positive as the rest of them, at the very least her tone had changed to being thoughtful.

'You're not leaving us with much wiggle room there, Auntie.' Lydia sighed as she tossed aside several chunky scripts of *Les Misérables,* knowing they'd never be able to find anyone to sing 'Bring Him Home' as well as Alfie Boe.

'Maybe it's useless.' Bam put her head in her hands, and even her curls seemed to droop with disappointment.

'Never!' said Layton, peering in through the doorway.

'It's not useless, Bam. We just haven't found an idea as brilliant as you, yet. But we will,' Morris said, slipping his hand into his auntie's.

'Think, Theo. Think!' Theo willed himself, rapping himself on the head with his knuckles.

'A story that everyone knows but that no one's seen on stage before,' Marigold said, opening her notebook in a small clear space on one of the desks and clicking her pen over and over to help her think.

'We need a story that feels familiar but not so familiar it's boring.' Bam finally turned to them all, her curls bouncing a little now. Marigold tapped her pen on the last page she'd been scrawling on, when suddenly a shadow fell across it.

'Marigold, what's that?'

'What's what?' Marigold squealed and instinctively lifted her feet off the floor, expecting a mouse to run into view for Mack to chase.

'That. Right there. In your notebook.' Bam was about to point to something but Marigold quickly slammed its pages shut.

'Nothing!' She held it close to her chest.

'That wasn't nothing.' Bam's smile finally returned. 'You're writing a play. She's writing a play, everyone! Children, children, she's writing a play!' She clapped her hands together and beamed at Marigold so hard it made her blush.

'I'm not! It's nothing, I promise!' Marigold looked down at her shuffling feet.

'Child, you're not in trouble!' Bam held her shoulders and gently shook her. 'Don't act like you're hiding a copy of Donald Trump's autobiography! You're being creative! That's something to share and be very, *very* proud of.'

'It really is nothing, though . . .' Marigold wished her hair was as long as Mabel's, because she would have loved nothing more than to disappear.

'Can we ask what it's about?' Dante enquired.

'I know what it's about!' Morris's hand shot up into the air, almost poking Lydia in the eye.

'How do *you* know?' Marigold snapped.

'Yes, Morris, how do *you* know?' Bam probed.

'Because it was *my* idea. You're writing about the Fossils, aren't you?' When Marigold didn't answer, Bam held out her hand for the notebook and, with a shaky hand, Marigold handed it over. Bam began flipping through the pages slowly, with her eyebrows knitted together. Then the pages started moving faster and faster until all of a sudden Bam erupted into thunderous laughter.

'*MY CLEVER GIRL!*' Bam boomed louder than the Pebbles had ever heard her. Her pride was even louder than when she was angry. When Lydia and the three children looked at Bam with puzzled expressions, Bam laughed even harder. 'Don't you see? Marigold is going to save the theatre with her brilliant, brilliant writing!'

'I . . . I am?' Marigold stammered. Bam knelt so close to her that Marigold could smell her orange blossom perfume.

'The tale of the Fossil sisters is the perfect story for our show.' She smiled.

'It's not a story everyone knows though . . .' said Morris.

'But it's a story that *should* be told . . .' said Bam

'. . . and it's a story that no one has ever seen on stage before . . .' said Mabel.

'. . . and it's familiar but couldn't possibly be boring!' finished Lydia.

'Marigold, my girl, you've done it!' Bam shrieked.

'But . . . but . . . I'm not a writer!'

'Of course you are. You're writing, aren't you?'

'Well, yes,' Marigold muttered.

'And do you like what you've written?'

'Well, no . . .' Marigold admitted, but Bam only nodded more.

'See! You're a writer!'

'But how will I know if I'm good enough?'

'You never will unless you keep writing and showing people your work. Come on, Marigold. We have a real shot here at saving this theatre, because you're a little genius. We'll all help with research, won't we?' The family nodded. 'I'm sure Lady at the library would love to lend a helping hand. Our little Pebble family theatre will all chip in, too.'

'Go on, Marigold,' encouraged Lydia.

'You can do it, Marigold!' Morris cheered.

'I believe in you, Marigold.' Mabel smiled, from behind her glossy mane. Marigold looked at the hope-filled eyes of her nearest and dearest. The people who always picked her up if she fell, promising now to lift her higher than ever before. Marigold took an extremely deep breath.

'OK. I'll do it,' she said finally, and she couldn't help but smile even though there seemed to be a hundred butterflies in her tummy that were desperate to flutter out. Lydia, Mabel and Morris cheered and applauded, but no one's voice was louder than Bam's booming '*HURRAH!*'

'Oh, my sweet, brilliant girl! We need a title right away so we can start telling everyone about our show!'

'Let's not get ahead of ourselves, Aunt Maude! She's only just agreed to write it!' Lydia warned.

'Ah, yes! We can think of a title later. Not too much later, though! We've only got just over five weeks to get it written, rehearsed and open.'

'Bam . . .' Lydia gasped, as everyone else's mouths fell open. 'Is that even possible?'

'Not only is it possible, Lydia, but, in this fickle, fast and fabulous business, I've seen it done in less. By the looks of it, Marigold is already halfway there! She's got seasoned pros

120

around her who will help to hone and tweak her talent where needs be, but I can tell she's a natural. Up to the challenge, Marigold?' Marigold thought she might throw up in one of the boxes, but she nodded quickly before she could talk herself out of it.

'Oh, Marigold! You're going to be marvellous. A star, I tell you, a star!' Bam hauled Marigold on to her feet, which was quite a feat for a woman with a back as bad as Brilliant Aunt Maude's, and whirled her round.

'I really will need everyone's help, though!' Marigold giggled. 'Maybe quite a lot of it.'

'That's what families are for, Marigold. We're right behind you. Every step of the way.' Lydia wrapped her arms round Marigold, then Mabel and Morris wrapped their arms round Lydia – and Bam wrapped her arms round them all. Marigold felt warm and cosy at the centre, but the moment was broken by Morris clearing his throat quite loudly.

'Of course, this is all very moving, but, if this works out and we do indeed manage to save our lovely theatre, I just want to make sure that everyone remembers that it was *aaaaaall* my idea.'

# 16

## No Room for Worry

It had been such an awfully exciting day. Lydia had made cheese-and-pickle sandwiches for lunch, and they'd all sat in a circle on the floor of the dressing room with boxes and scripts and scores. It was a lovely picnic and they talked for what felt like hours about the play Marigold was going to write, although Marigold had kept very quiet. As it had been such a special day, the children had been allowed to stay up a little later than usual. Marigold, Mabel and Morris were all sitting cross-legged on Marigold's bed, nestling mugs of hot chocolate in their laps and cautiously sipping it through mountains of whipped cream and clouds of marshmallow, too eager to wait for it to cool.

'Where are you going to start, Marigold? With your story?' Morris asked, bouncing up and down slightly with excitement.

'Morris, will you stop jiggling about. You're making my drink spill . . . *Oh no!*' As Mabel reached over to place a steadying hand on his shoulder, a little piece of her hair swept across the cream and turned from red to white. Mack saw his opportunity while Mabel was distracted. He jumped on to the bed and stuck his little whiskered face into the cream in her mug, hurriedly licking up as much as he could before anyone noticed.

'Gross . . .' Morris said with a disgusted grin.

'I'm not too sure yet,' Marigold said, returning to the matter at hand. She swept an arm underneath Mack and lifted him on to the floor in one smooth motion. He scarpered from the room before anyone could give him a telling off and Mabel put her drink to one side on the floor with a huff and a pout.

'I'm going to need to find out a lot more about the Fossil sisters before I write anything else.' Marigold took a big sip of her too-hot hot chocolate, burning her tongue slightly but not wanting to talk any more about the ginormous task that awaited her.

'It's *my* turn to read tonight – about Posy,' Morris said, reaching for the journal that lay on the duvet between them.

'Careful you don't spill your drink on it! Maybe I should hold it for you . . .' Mabel said, seizing Morris's mug from him and taking a sip. Morris didn't seem to notice now that he was fumbling through the pages of the journal, looking for Posy's entry.

'Here we are!' His eyes lit up as he found Posy's messy but bold handwriting. 'Ready?' Morris asked, and his sisters nodded.

'Knock, knock . . .' Lydia interrupted, tapping on the door with Bam peering in over her shoulder. 'We were wondering if maybe we could join you for this special reading of the Fossils' journal. Now that we're in on the secret, that is.' The Pebble children nodded, and they all squeezed on to the bed together until there was very little room left.

'This is awfully exciting. I've not heard anything about Pauline, Petrova and Posy for so long,' said Bam.

'Let's hope everyone else feels the same and buys a ticket to our show when it's ready,' Lydia chimed.

'They'll be keen as mustard when they hear! Just you wait!' Bam squeaked.

'Shh!' Marigold hushed them abruptly, cutting through their excited chatter. 'It's Morris's turn to read.' Lydia and Bam exchanged a look over the children's heads and shrugged. Lydia put her arms round Marigold and it took a few moments before she finally warmed into the embrace and snuggled against Lydia.

'Are we all comfortable?' Morris asked.

'I haven't sat cross-legged in about thirty years or so,' Bam said, shifting from left to right and back again as she tried to find a comfortable spot. 'You'll need to read very quickly, or my legs might fall asleep forever and they'll need to be cut off so . . . off you go.' Morris giggled and then began.

January 2nd 1940
Hello from Czechoslovakia and Happy New Year! Well, I seem to be somewhat of a triumph. Manoff, my excellent new teacher, says I'm head and shoulders above the rest in my class. In talent, of course. I'm still a little short for my age but I'd settle for talent over height any day.

'She seems a little . . . sure of herself?' Morris said, his face twisting into a wince.

'Sometimes a little certainty in your own talent goes a long way, Morris. It makes people pay attention when they otherwise wouldn't.' Lydia gave Marigold's shoulders a squeeze.

'As long as one doesn't get too big for one's boots, a bit of self-confidence in the world of entertainment doesn't go unnoticed.' Bam agreed, peering over the top of her glasses and locking eyes with Marigold for the briefest of moments before nudging Morris to carry on.

'Hmm . . .' Marigold hummed, unconvinced. But it wasn't heard as Morris had continued to read with gusto.

Nana definitely seems to be struggling with the adjustment. She's constantly moaning about the food and seems to be awfully troubled that she can't find oatmeal for porridge or treacle for puddings. She daren't try anything new, but I find the cuisine to be much to my liking. I've sent some cake along with the journal to you, Pauline, and I'll bring some back with me the next time I visit London for you, Petrova. It's called 'bublanina'. This one has raspberries in it, but sometimes it has blueberries or apricots and it's my favourite of all the things I've tried. I can never eat too much of it before a rehearsal though or I start to feel a bit queasy. I learnt that the hard way!

'Oh, how I wish we could try some!' Morris said, his tummy gurgling at the thought of something as delicious as bublanina.

'It does sound rather yummy, doesn't it?' Bam agreed. 'I wonder if we could find somewhere to purchase some in London . . .'

'*I have some exciting news*,' said Morris suddenly.

'Oh, really? You've kept that quiet!' Mabel laughed.

'No! I mean Posy!' he said, flapping the journal at her. 'Listen . . .'

I have some exciting news. Monsieur Manoff came to me after rehearsals the other day and said, 'Posy!' . . . He speaks very dramatically in his French accent if you can imagine it. 'I am taking this company to America. Before that happens, you will be dancing for me. I plan two new ballets written specially for you.' Isn't it marvellous? Two new ballets written specially for me! Can you quite believe it! Pauline, you're the reason I am here. If you hadn't signed that Hollywood contract and used the money to send me to Czechoslovakia, there's no way I'd be dancing in two ballets of my own and heading for New York. I'm scared I didn't express my gratitude enough when we were in London. I fear I behaved in a rather spoilt way, but I hope you agree that it is never too late to mend one's wicked ways. Thank you, dearest sister, from the bottom of my heart. Thank you, thank you, thank you.

Petrova, I loved the photograph you sent, so here's one of me in rehearsals that Monsieur Manoff took so I could see my posture and make it better next time. If you look carefully, you can see Nana scowling in the background! Your turn to send a photograph, Pauline. Make it a good one!

Love to you both.

Your littlest sister,
Posy
X


They all leant in round Morris to get a good look at the photograph Posy had sent. It was black-and-white, of course, but she was wearing a light-coloured leotard, tights and pointe shoes.

'They're really hard to dance in!' Morris said, gesturing to her perfectly pointed feet. 'Only the best dancers can dance in those. It takes years' worth of practice.'

'How is she managing to stay up like that?' Mabel gasped.

'Clearly Posy was born to dance,' Marigold said.

'Like Morris here.' Bam grinned down at him.

'Do you really think so?'

'Are you kidding?' Bam seized Morris's feet and pulled them towards her, sending Morris on to his back and giggling all the while. 'These feet,' she said, kissing each one in turn, 'although very smelly, were made to dance. Just like Marigold's imagination was made to write and Mabel's brain was made to out-think everyone else in the room.'

'You're a brave woman, Bam! I wash his socks and I don't think I've ever smelt anything quite like it.' Lydia held her nose and they all laughed.

'Yes, I'm quite regretting it now.' Bam mimed a gag which sent them all into further hysterics. 'All right, it's time to settle down and drift off to dreamland, anyway. Into bed, the lot of you!' Bam began to lift their quilts, each in turn, until the right Pebble got into bed underneath it and she could tuck them in. Once Lydia had turned out the light and the door was closed, she looked at Bam and sighed.

'They're the best thing that's ever happened to me.' Lydia couldn't help smiling from ear to ear.

'And me.' Bam sniffed, unable to contain her emotions.

'And this theatre. Do you really think they can save it? They're just children, Bam.' Lydia rubbed her tired and slightly weepy eyes with her hands and shook her head.

'There's no "*just*" about it.' Bam began to creep away from the children's door, knowing they might overhear a conversation they weren't meant to be a part of. 'Children are often brighter than the lot of us grown-ups put together. They naturally think outside the box. That is, until the world squashes them back into their box, and then it's so hard for them to climb out again. It has never crossed my mind that our three Pebbles aren't capable of anything they set their minds to. And right now all they can think about is saving our lovely theatre.'

'But five weeks, Bam . . .' Lydia rubbed her temples. Bam held up a hand to stop her worrying in its tracks.

'I know. I know you don't think I realize what a challenge it will be, but it was only a matter of hours ago that we'd completely given up. The children want to try and, although there's only a slim chance, it's still a chance. One single lottery ticket still might win the millions. One tiny spark might just ignite a fire.'

'And if it doesn't work?' Lydia's eyelids were heavy and beginning to droop. Bam placed her hands on her niece's cheeks and gave them a gentle squeeze like she used to when Lydia was little.

'We still have each other.' Bam smiled.

'If you're sure.' Lydia yawned, exhaustion from the long day finally setting in.

'I'd be very silly not to be sure. Listen, Lydia.' Bam took her by the shoulders and gave her a gentle shake. 'Those three can only achieve whatever they're going to achieve if we believe in them. And I mean *really* believe. Not pretend-believe to make them feel better about themselves. This theatre has no room for doubt.'

'I have no doubt they can do it, I just . . . worry.'

'Ah. Now that's different,' Bam said. 'Even if this theatre had no room for worry, I don't think worry would care all that much and it would move in anyway. Good thing is, you can still get things done while worrying. But doubt? Doubt's an ambition-killer. So, let's close the door on it.' Lydia nodded. 'Tonight.'

# 17

## A New Show in Town

The theatre was buzzing. Dante was filled with vim and vigour and was already planning simple yet effective stage illusions before he'd even read Marigold's script. Dawson, however, said nothing – but his eyebrow did rise, which Dante promised was a good sign. Cora and Layton were also very excited about the new plan but had a few concerns to express to the theatre owner.

'Bam, with all these new-fangled ideas and the young 'uns taking things over, as rightfully they should . . . is there still a place for us?' Cora took her husband's hand and held it close to her heart, while Bam's heart almost broke cleanly in two.

'I shall hear no more of such nonsense,' she said sharply. 'This theatre has never been just a theatre, has it? It's a home for people who love it as much as I do. We are family. You always have a place here. Now, no more silliness. You have a new show to get to grips with; I'm sure Marigold has lines you'll need to learn.' Bam shooed them away, but only because a lump was forming in her throat that she was sure would turn into a sob if she continued looking at their worried expressions. She spotted Morris peering over the back of a seat, and her face quickly changed into a grin. She galloped over to him like an overexcited pony. 'The question is, what are *you* up to?' She gently prodded his nose with the tip of her red fingernail, and he giggled.

'I'm just so excited!' Morris stood and began to bounce up and down with his feet pointed perfectly as they lifted into the air. People were already taking down the set from the last show (which no one had come to see) and the brand-new set was being built and painted. 'Our very own show!' Morris squealed. 'With music and dancing and lights and dancing and sets and dancing . . .'

'Morris, my boy,' Bam said gently, putting a hand on his shoulders to ground him just for a moment. 'Our show isn't a musical, so I can't imagine there being much need for any choreography.'

'But *BAAAAAM*!' he moaned. 'Posy was a *ballerina*! She *danced*! Someone is going to have to dance at some point in the show. Whoever plays her will have to know the right steps. You can't leave that kind of thing to chance. It's all about the detail!'

'Ah, yes. I suppose you're right,' Bam said. 'Well, I'm sure you, Claudia and Kitty will be able to whip something up, won't you?' She smiled and Morris's eyes widened.

'I'm . . . I'm in charge of choreography?' He gulped.

'Well, I don't see why not! You're up to the challenge, aren't you?'

'Yes! Oh, yes, I am! We can have a big dance number that everyone joins in, and tutus and pointe shoes and –'

'Remember, we are on a budget, Morris. Think small and simple.'

'Got it. Small and simple . . . and *amazing*!' he added, before twirling away, yelling for Claudia and Kitty to come as quickly as they could.

Mabel gently knocked on Dawson's dressing-room door hoping to find Dante, but Dawson told her he was in the cellar.

'W-what's he doing d-down there?' Mabel shuddered. The Pebble children *never* went down to the cellar. When the Pebbles were little, Lydia was horrified to find out that Bam had completely misjudged which bedtime stories to tell. She once found her telling a very young Marigold, Mabel and Morris about a theatre in the West End that had a body buried within the walls of its cellar. The ghost of the unfortunate person would wander the corridors and wreak havoc if it didn't think an actor was very good. The children never really visited the theatre's cellar at that time anyway. They had never thought about it much before then. But, after Bam told them that story, it was *all* they thought about for a very long time. Instead of never minding the cellar, now they actively avoided it – and the mere mention of it could stir up terrifying thoughts and sometimes even nightmares.

'Illusions,' Dawson said, and politely waited for her to shuffle down the corridor before closing the door. Mabel sucked in all her fear, blew it all out in one big breath and made her way to the Pebble Theatre's cellar.

'Dante . . .' she called out from the top of the tiny, winding spiral staircase. It was painted black, but the paint crackled and peeled off under her hand. She couldn't see the bottom of the stairs through the thick black blanket of darkness. It didn't seem like there was any room for light down there at all. *Maybe that's because the ghosts suck the light from the room so you can't see them when they eat you*, said Mabel's brain. 'DANTE!' she called out louder, sure he couldn't be down there, when suddenly a beam of yellow light shattered the darkness.

'Mabel? Is that you?' said Dante's deep voice. 'Come on down. I'm just working on something.' Mabel's heart was thudding in her chest, but she descended the steps all the same. *If Dante is down there, how scary can it be?* When Dante's torch guided her feet down the stairs, she could see he was busy at work on the far side of the room.

'Stay there a second,' he said, and promptly turned off his torch, plunging them into darkness. Mabel let out a little whimper but quickly stifled her fear by putting her hands over her mouth. Slowly, golden light seeped into the cellar and Dante appeared again.

'What do you think?' he said, grinning from ear to ear and clearly very proud of himself.

'What do I think?' Mabel asked through her fingers. 'Of what?'

'Come closer to me.' Dante was standing in the corner of the room and with every step she took towards him Mabel realized that he looked transparent, as if she could put her hand right through him.

'You look like a ghost!' Mabel said. She reached out to touch him and found that her hand bumped up against a cool, crystal-clear pane of glass. She snatched her hand back and Dante laughed, but the sound came from behind her. Mabel whipped round and saw that Dante was hidden in a corner of the room behind a wall, so she couldn't have seen him when she first walked in. There were several big theatre lights at his feet pointed up at him.

'And a ghost I am! It's a magic trick! Maybe one of the oldest theatre illusions there is. It's called *Pepper's Ghost*. Clever, eh?' Dante beamed.

'It's so cool! How does it work?'

'It's all about angles and lighting. If you angle the glass just right and light yourself, or whatever you want, you can create a ghost.'

'That's amazing, Dante, really, but . . . there aren't any ghosts in Marigold's story,' she said gently.

'Oh, indeed? That's a shame. Well, never mind. I've got lots of magic up my sleeve that I'm sure we can find a good use for.' Dante switched off the lights with a sad click. Mabel watched the ghost of Dante disappear and, just like that, the magic was over. 'No sour faces. I've just taught you a way to absolutely terrify your brother and sister.' Dante winked. 'Now, let's figure out what magic we *can* use in Marigold's story.'

The hammering and drilling was so loud that Marigold could hear it from two floors up in the spare dressing room, where all the old props, scripts and scores were stored. Bam had very kindly said she could use it as her writing room. The idea of having an official office was awfully exciting, and Marigold thought it meant she was going to be able to write a huge amount, and very quickly, without her brother and sister or anyone else able to distract her. As it turned out, everything seemed so much louder when you were left on your own. Her thoughts were drowned out by the sound of people chatting as they passed the theatre below. The purring of Mack in the corner and even the constant tick-tock of the clock made it impossible to think. Even when she drew the curtains, gently shooed Mack from the room and took the batteries out of the wall clock, the silence became suffocating.

'*Urgh*,' Marigold groaned and slumped her head on the desk. She didn't even have a title, yet! This was going to be a lot harder than she thought.

# 18

## A Visit to Wonderland

'How's the writing coming along, Marigold?' Lydia asked gently, adding another book to the mountain on Marigold's table at the library. Half a week had slipped by without anyone noticing. With only four weeks left to go, the whole gang had taken a research trip to help the writing process along. Marigold sat taking notes from books and writing what she could, while everyone else scoured the shelves for anything that might help. Cora and Layton were trying to find books on acting, flying and dancing. Theo was looking for books about the 1940s, and Dante and Dawson were on the hunt for books about strong women throughout history, although Dante kept getting distracted by books about Houdini. Mabel and Morris had been sent to do research on the library's computer after they'd added the book *Playwriting for Dummies* to Marigold's pile, which she didn't find funny at all. Lady was darting about between them all, helping as best she could to locate everything the library had to offer. Marigold didn't like to say anything, but she was very distracted by the sound of Lady's heels clip-clopping on the library's wooden floor.

'It's going fine,' Marigold said, closing her notebook and hiding its mainly blank pages.

'Just fine?' Lydia probed, but Marigold simply shrugged.

'She's barely written anything,' Mabel said, throwing a scrunched-up piece of paper at her sister's head.

'That's not true!' Marigold protested. 'Besides, how would you know!'

'You left your notebook open when you went to the toilet and I . . . I . . . might have had a peek.'

'Mabel!' Marigold slammed her fists down on the table and was quickly hushed by three or four people who were hidden among the shelves.

'Mabel, that wasn't very nice of you,' Lydia said. 'Is that true though, Marigold? Are you struggling a little bit? Because you know that's OK, don't you? No one expects you to do this all on your own?'

'Really?'

'Oh, Marigold. I told Bam this was going to be too much pressure.'

'It's not! I promise!'

'Why don't we hire a writer instead?'

'I *am* a writer,' said Marigold, pouting.

'Not if you don't write anything . . .' Mabel scoffed.

'Mabel, that's enough!' Lydia scolded her.

'I really can do this, Lydia. I swear I can. I've just got writer's block, that's all.'

'Well, what can we do to help?'

'Do you think there's anyone still alive who knew the Fossils?' asked Marigold.

'Bam knew them,' Lydia replied.

'She was only very little, though. Is there anyone who knew them *properly*?'

'They'd be very old if there was. In their nineties, I should imagine.'

Marigold looked down at her notebook and fiddled with her pencil. 'But I'm sure we could look into it. If anyone would know, it's Bam.'

Back at the theatre, Lydia and Marigold went in search of Bam.

'Hmm, the only person I know who might still be knocking about is Winifred. She went to the same stage school as the Fossils. Not sure she'd take too kindly to being asked questions about them, though. I got the sense there was a little bit of rivalry between Pauline and Winifred back in the day. Not that she ever said as much. She just got very tense whenever Pauline's name was mentioned.' Bam was sitting behind her desk in her office. This is where she looked most like the businesswoman she was, and Marigold couldn't quite see past the professional exterior to her mad, loving aunt underneath. Then she spotted her aunt's blue fluffy slippers tucked under the desk and Marigold was pleased. The illusion was shattered.

'How did you know Winifred?' asked Marigold.

'She gave up acting in the end, to become an agent for other actors. Cast some wonderful people in a show for me. Oof, that was an awfully long time ago now. I'm not sure she'd even remember me.' Bam took a moment to think, weighing up the pros and cons in her mind. Marigold got the sense Bam needed a bit of convincing.

'Oh, please, Brilliant Aunt Maude? Do it for the theatre?' Marigold laced her fingers and held her hands under her chin, praying to the theatre gods that Bam would grant her wish.

'It couldn't hurt to try,' Lydia said gently. 'Especially if it makes a difference to Marigold's story.'

'A big difference!' Marigold added.

'And as long as Marigold doesn't outstay her welcome and doesn't push too hard.'

'Just a few simple questions,' Marigold promised.

'All right, all right, I'll make some calls. How can I resist those big eyes of yours, eh?' Bam picked up the receiver of her bright-red desk phone, pulled out a diary from her desk and flicked to the page on which Winifred's office number was scrawled. Bam's red nails jabbed at the numbers on the phone. Marigold could hear it ringing but Bam put her fingers over the end of the phone so that no one could hear her if they picked up, and said, 'Do we have a title? Just so I can let her know . . .' Bam asked hopefully, but her answer came in the form of Marigold hanging her head and looking at her shoes. 'No matter! No matter! But remember, Marigold, if she's still alive she'll be in her nineties. If you thought I was doddery and forgetful, she's at least a decade older than I am so . . . be gentle.' Marigold grinned and crossed her heart.

As it turned out, Winifred was still very much alive and her acting agency was thriving. Bam and Marigold stood together, hand in hand, in front of a painted black door in central London, where a bronze plaque shone in the early morning sunlight. It said WONDERLAND LTD in bold capital letters, and underneath was a keypad and a speaker. It had several buttons – some numbered, some coloured – and Marigold caught Bam staring at it as if it had come from a different planet altogether.

'Maybe try the button with the picture of a bell on it?' Marigold suggested, pointing towards a big, round white button near the bottom of the keypad in the centre.

'A bell? Why a bell?' Bam huffed, still staring at the other buttons intently in case there was something she had missed.

'Because . . . it's a doorbell?' Marigold was so nervous about meeting with Winifred from Wonderland Ltd that Bam's faffing was putting her even more on edge.

'Well, all these different gizmos are far too much nonsense. Whatever happened to just the one button for one bell.' Bam struggled, her nail slipping on the smooth polished metal so that Marigold quickly obliged and pushed it for her. It rang twice.

'Welcome to Wonderland, how may I help you?' said a pleasant muffled voice through the speaker.

'HELLO! WE'RE HERE TO MEET WITH WINIFRED.' Bam crouched and shouted at completely the wrong part of the speaker.

'Sorry? I can't quite hear you,' said the voice.

'WINIFRED! WE ARE HERE TO SEE HER,' Bam yelled more slowly.

'Do you have an appointment? She's very much in demand so if you don't have an appointment I can't help you.' The voice sounded clipped and impatient. Marigold gently pushed her aunt aside and spoke directly into the speaker.

'We have an appointment. Cooper and Pebble. Nine forty-five.'

'Ah, yes. I see it here. Come on up to the fifth floor.'

'Well done, Marigold,' Bam said. 'Did I just show my age a little bit?'

'Maybe a little.' Marigold laughed.

'Don't laugh too hard.' Bam smirked. 'Before you know it, you'll blink and it'll be you standing here fumbling with new-fangled technology that probably doesn't even exist yet!' And, with that, a buzzer buzzed and Bam pushed open the door.

When they reached the fifth floor, the rooms were painted from floor to ceiling almost entirely in white and all the furniture was white to match. There were white desks, white lamps, white computers, white vases filled with white flowers, white sofas with white cushions, and the only things hanging on the walls were black-and-white photographs in painted white frames. The receptionist was also dressed from head to toe in a white trouser suit with a white headset to match.

'Hello. Please take a seat. Winifred is just in another meeting.'

'I'll stand, if it's all the same to you,' said Bam. 'The colour white and I don't really get along. If I'm left around it for any time at all, it seems to no longer be white – expert spiller, me. Marigold, you go ahead.'

'It's OK,' said Marigold, who was far too nervous to sit still. She fiddled with her hair, bit the skin round her nails until her fingers were sore, and paced up and down and all round Bam who remained perfectly still.

'Look, Bam!' Marigold said suddenly, noticing that one of

the photos hanging on the wall was of the Fossil sister they had come to talk about. 'It's Pauline!'

'And Winifred. That's her there on the left.'

'They don't look like rivals.' The picture was of two teenagers with their arms round each other, grinning madly at the camera.

'Winifred will see you now,' the receptionist said without looking up. 'Room one. Turn left and then follow the corridor all the way to the end. You won't be able to miss it.'

The walls along the hallway were also adorned with black-and-white photos, mostly of Winifred on red carpets or on stage – in shows, mid-scene, looking anguished, crying or kissing a leading man. From the looks of it, she'd had quite a career herself.

Marigold looked away and saw that towards the end of the corridor, there was a white door. On the frosted glass the words THE RABBIT HOLE were etched.

'Ever the theatrical!' said Bam, stifling a laugh. 'I think this is us. Shall I do the honours?' Bam asked, raising her hand. Marigold nodded and Bam gently knocked on the door. A voice on the other side trilled, '*Coooome iii-iiinnn!*' Bam turned the doorknob and pushed on the pure white wood. What lay beyond took their breath away . . .

# 19

## A Colourful Personality

'Come in! Come in! How lovely to meet you, Maude!'

'Actually, we've met before although it was a long time –'

'Marigold! Don't you look lovely in your pretty coat and hat?' If Winifred was almost a decade older than Brilliant Aunt Maude, it certainly didn't show. Winifred practically leapt out of her swivel chair and bounced over to her guests, embracing them both in one go and planting great big kisses on their cheeks, leaving behind bright pink lipstick marks. Her nails matched her bright pink, poker-straight hair, which was styled into a bob with sharp edges that cut into her chin. She wore thick green horn-rimmed glasses, and a blue leotard with matching tights. When Marigold looked at her feet, she was also wearing blue trainers with weights strapped round her ankles.

'You look very . . . active,' said Bam, looking down at her own snuggly jumper and coat. She'd never worn anything like what Winifred was sporting and she was sure she'd look silly if she did – but, somehow, Winifred pulled it off.

'When you plan on living forever, Maude, you've got to stay fit and healthy!' Winifred herself wasn't the only splash of colour in the room, though . . . oh, no! It was as if Winifred's office had sucked the colour out of the entire building and spat it out all over itself. The desk was green, the carpet was blue, the curtains were pink, and the walls were burgundy. Winifred had trinkets, lamps, statues and cushions dotted about the room in purples, oranges and yellows. Marigold glanced sideways at Bam, who was wide-eyed, unblinking, unable to do anything except drink in the rainbow before her.

'Sit down! Sit down! Make yourselves at home. Coffee? Tea? Gin?' Winifred clinked two tumblers together with enthusiasm and an enticing raise of the eyebrows.

'Umm . . .' Bam hesitated. Marigold knew that if she wasn't here her aunt would jump at the latter offer, but instead Bam said, 'Tea will do nicely, thank you.'

'Tea for me, too, please,' Marigold mumbled.

'Sorry, I didn't quite catch that, young 'un?' Winifred cupped her hand round her ear and shut her eyes tight, as if that would help her hear better. Marigold cleared her throat and could feel beads of sweat begin to form on her brow.

'I'd like tea, too,' she said, louder this time. Almost a little too loud, and Bam flinched. 'Please. Thank you. Please,' Marigold added hysterically.

'There we go! That's better! No one likes a mumbler.' Winifred swapped the glass tumblers for china teacups adorned with intricate blue floral patterns. 'How do you take it?'

'No milk, four sugars,' said Bam. Winifred paused above the sugar bowl and mouthed 'Four?' at Marigold, even though Bam could clearly see. Marigold simply nodded – she was used to Bam's odd habits.

'Milk and one sugar for me, please. Thank you,' Marigold said as clearly and loudly as she could.

'Oh, such a polite child! Polite people go far.' Winifred smiled as she flipped the purple kettle on and clinked a teaspoon against the sugar bowl as she dished heaps of sugar out into the delicate cups. 'But don't be a pushover,' she growled, jabbing the teaspoon in Marigold's direction. 'No one likes a pushover. But don't be too boisterous either. You can't go about throwing your weight around like a cow in a candy store, no, no. You need to be tactful.' Marigold's head started to whirl. She felt she should be taking notes, but she also had the overwhelming urge to correct Winifred's mistake. It was supposed to be 'a bull in a china shop' and 'a kid in a candy store' – but Bam put an encouraging hand on her shoulder and instead Marigold bit her tongue, knowing she needed to make the best impression because otherwise her play would never be finished.

'Spoken like an agent who's had to do some damage control in her time!' Bam used her fake laugh. Marigold knew this because it was the same laugh she used when Mabel told a joke that definitely wasn't funny.

Winifred finally gave them their tea.

'You don't mind if I . . . ?' She didn't finish her sentence and neither Marigold nor Bam had any idea what she wanted to do. Smoke? Have a tumbler of gin while they sipped their tea? Both of them nodded, none the wiser. Winifred reached under her desk and when she reappeared she was holding small pink weights in her hands. She bounced up on to her feet and began to run round her office, lifting the weights up and down above her head.

'So,' she panted, 'what was it . . . you both . . . wanted to see me for?' Marigold glanced at Bam, only to discover her aunt's face had almost turned as blue as Winifred's outfit from desperately trying not to giggle. Seeing her aunt's struggle made Marigold's own attempt to keep a straight face even harder. Winifred's eccentricity seemed to know no bounds.

'Marigold here has a few questions, and we were hoping maybe you'd be able to answer some of them.' Bam nudged Marigold with her elbow and gave her a wink. Marigold opened her rucksack and pulled out her notebook.

'How charming! Is it for a school project? Are you an aspiring actress?' Winifred tried to look over to Marigold, but then almost ran into the coatrack in the corner of the room. Bam whimpered, biting the inside of her cheeks but failing to keep from smiling. Marigold, however, stayed silent.

'Go on, Marigold,' Bam encouraged.

'Sorry, I'm just . . . erm . . .'

'Ahh, is this a classic case of stage fright?' Winifred puffed.

'Something like that.' Marigold blushed. 'It's just . . . I get made fun of by my classmates for asking too many questions. I'm not used to someone actually *wanting* me to ask lots of questions.'

'Oh, my dear.' Winifred slowed to a stop in front of Marigold and shook her head so violently her pink bob swished and the ends got stuck in her pink lipstick. 'Why do you think my whole office is based on *Alice in Wonderland*, hmm?'

'Well . . . isn't that the show you were in when you were a child? Where your love of theatre began?'

'It was, yes. Someone's done their research!' Winifred said to Bam, wide-eyed and impressed. 'It does hold a lot of sentimental value for me, but the *real* reason is that Alice was filled with curiosity.'

'Curiouser and curiouser,' Bam quoted.

'Exactly! Alice was so curious, in fact, that she fell down

the rabbit hole, discovered a whole new world and went on the biggest adventure of her life. Curiosity might be what killed the cat, but curiosity is also what gave the cat a jolly good time before she went!'

'Your classmates might not understand what it's like to have an active mind and a vibrant imagination,' Bam said. 'One day they'll get it but, if they don't, I pity the person who will never see the world the way that you do, Marigold.' Bam smiled down at her little Pebble, who suddenly sat up taller and clenched her notebook tighter.

'I'm writing a play,' Marigold said with conviction.

'A play?' Winifred cooed.

'It's a play for me, actually,' Bam interjected. 'She's an *exceptionally* good writer and so I've commissioned her to write a play for the Pebble.'

'How exciting!' Winifred's eyes flashed back to Marigold. 'Your debut! Always good to start them off young, Maude. Can I ask what it's about?' This was Marigold's moment. She took a breath.

'Well, that's why I've been dying to speak to you, actually. It's about the Fossil sisters. I've been able to find out so much already about Petrova and Posy Fossil, but Pauline still remains a bit of a mystery. Being able to talk to someone who actually knew her is quite amazing.' Marigold swallowed hard. Winifred was staring at her, and Marigold was certain that the more she stared the wider her eyes became. 'I – If there was anything you could tell me about her, anything at all, I'd be eternally grateful.' A silence filled the colourful office like smoke from a fire Marigold had lit with her request.

'Goodness me!' Winifred said, her face unchanging. 'I definitely didn't expect that.'

'Is . . . everything all right?' Bam asked.

'Of course! It's just a funny feeling, isn't it? Looking into the past.'

'Yes, I suppose it is.' Bam smiled, knowing the feeling well.

'You'll understand one day, Marigold. When you're as old as we are, you'll look back at who you are today and it'll feel like several decades have passed in the blink of an eye.' Winifred's eyes had glazed over, and she seemed to be lost somewhere other than her office. 'Sorry, I'm rambling. What did you want to know?'

'Were you and Pauline really rivals?' Marigold blurted it out so fast that all the words ran together.

'Oh, goodness no!' Winifred finally took a seat behind her desk. 'Well, sort of, but only as children when we didn't really know any better. We all wanted to play the best and biggest part we could, so you were taught to see everyone around you as competition. As you get older you realize there's just no room for such pettiness. You either get the part or you don't. Life moves on either way.'

'Roll with the punches!' Bam said.

'Exactly!'

'So, you were friends? I noticed that picture in the reception area.'

'Yes, we became good friends in the end. However, we didn't get to see each other very often. She travelled so much, and I stayed in London.'

'Did you keep in touch?' Marigold felt like she was on a roll now.

'It was a lot harder back then. No mobile phones, no internet, no instant messaging. But she did send me these.' Winifred opened a drawer in her desk and pulled out what looked like a photo album. When she opened it and passed it to Marigold, she saw that it was filled with postcards from all over the world.

'Wow . . .'

'Yes, they're quite a marvel. There's even one from Papua New Guinea in here. She sent so many over the years. So many arrived that in the end my children called her "Auntie Postcard". They never met her, but they wrote to her too when she was in one place for long enough to have an address.' Marigold flipped through the pages. There must have been over a hundred postcards. Words like 'Dear Friend' and 'Wish you were here!' jumped out at her. There was friendship and love in every word, and Marigold hated to think that the rivalry Winifred and Pauline shared when they were merely children might be the way they were remembered. 'You can

take them with you, if you like? A loan for your research.'
Marigold's face lit up, and Winifred couldn't help but laugh.
'Will they help?'

'More than you could know! Thank you, Winifred. Who
Pauline really was is the missing piece I've been looking for.'
Marigold closed the album and hugged it to her chest.

'Well, I've always been good at a jigsaw!'

'I promise I'll take good care of it.'

'I have no doubt! Oh, come here!' Winifred put her arms
round Marigold and for such a spindly woman she was
extraordinarily strong. Marigold could barely breathe in her
embrace.

'How can we ever thank you?' Bam asked before they left.

'I think a ticket to opening night should do it!' Winifred
winked, and sent them on their way.

# 20

## Mack Needs Help

Marigold and Bam made a pit stop for hot chocolate at their favourite cafe, wiping whipped cream from their top lips before returning to the theatre. They found the theatre in a state of uproar.

'It was in my room.' Theodore was sitting at the stage door, holding a flannel to his head with shaky hands. Petunia rubbed his shoulders and handed him a cup of tea, one eye covered by a giant feather that dangled down from a little peacock that was sitting at a jaunty angle on her head.

'Sweet tea is good for a shock. Drink up,' she said, tapping the bottom of the mug as he took a sip, causing it to spill out over the brim and dribble down his chin.

'Couldn't believe it when I saw it. I've come this far never having seen one and now . . . now this . . . !' He stopped talking abruptly before a sob erupted out of his mouth. Instead he held the flannel tight to his lips, but his eyes continued to water. Morris ran from inside the theatre and barrelled up to Theodore with wide eyes.

'Was it a ghost? Did you see one? What did it look like? Was it see-through? Was its head dangling off its shoulders?'

'Gross!' Marigold squirmed.

'Morris, that is quite enough,' Bam said firmly. 'Theodore, dearest, whatever is the matter? I didn't think you'd be the sort to be frightened of a little theatre ghost.'

'Not a ghost, Maude.' Theo shivered.

'Something worse than the dead come back to haunt us?' Bam gasped.

'*Much* worse,' he whimpered.

'My goodness, what on earth was it?'

'It was a . . . a . . . a *mouse*!' Theodore finally gave in to his emotions and burst into tears, his great, wide shoulders shuddering so hard that everyone with their consoling arms round him juddered along with him. Bam had to force herself not to roll her eyes. There had always been the odd mouse scurrying about the Pebble Theatre.

'Mice! Well, that's nothing that our Mack can't handle. That's why we've got him. And I don't think a London theatre can call itself a theatre without a few little mice.'

'Actually, Bam,' said Lydia, appearing with Mabel in the doorway, 'I think even Mack would be overwhelmed.'

'Oh, no!' squealed Theodore. 'You haven't found more?!' He lifted his big boots off the floor and desperately looked about for any more furry visitors.

'Nothing to worry about, Theo!' Lydia said with a bright smile but then, with a meaningful widening of the eyes, she added, 'Bam, a word?'

Bam, Morris and Marigold shuffled through into the theatre, closing the door on the sound of Theodore's inconsolable sobbing.

'How bad is it?'

'They're everywhere, Bam. Mack is having a marvellous time of it but even he can't keep up with just how many there are. It's like they're multiplying by the second!' Lydia wiped her brow and moved her headset away from her ear for a moment. Suddenly they could hear lots of squealing through the earphones. 'Everyone's gone a bit mad.'

'What do we do?' Mabel said, looking down at the carpet and then jumping at her own shadow, thinking it was a mouse following close behind her.

'Traps?' Morris suggested.

'I'm not killing anything,' Bam insisted.

'What about those ultrasonic devices that keep the mice away?'

'You'd need one for every single dressing room and corridor in the theatre, but I think I've got a better idea . . .' Suddenly, Bam's face broke into a grin that spread from ear to ear and rattled her dangly earrings. Marigold, Mabel and Morris had no idea what it meant, but Lydia had already begun to shake her head.

'Bam. No.'

'Lydia. Yes.' Bam had already turned on her heels and was heading back through the stage door and out of the theatre.

'One is enough!' Lydia said. The Pebble children all looked at each other, completely baffled.

'Clearly not! Marigold, Morris, get your coats!'

'What about me?!'

'I need you here with me, Mabel.' Lydia sighed, giving into Bam and this mysterious idea she'd had. Mabel pouted. 'Dante said you've got some tricks up your sleeve for the show. Can I see?' Lydia asked. Mabel's pout quickly dissolved into a smile as she took Lydia by the hand and led her down into the cellar of the Pebble Theatre.

'Brilliant Aunt Maude . . .' Morris said as he ran to catch up with his aunt, shrugging his coat on as he went. Their aunt might have been quite old, but at the pace she was walking Marigold and Morris were certain she'd give Mo Farah a challenge if she broke into a run. 'As you are so utterly brilliant, I'm sure that you're taking us somewhere equally as brilliant as you but . . . are we allowed to know where?' Morris gave her his best puppy-dog eyes, but she didn't even glance down. Instead, a little smile appeared at the corners of her mouth.

'We're so very almost there, Morris. I promise you it won't be long before you work it out.'

'Can we guess?' Marigold asked, putting her arm round her little brother.

'If you must,' Bam said over her shoulder, as Marigold and Morris fell behind her to conspire.

'OK. The theatre is full of mice,' Morris whispered.

'Mice we need to get rid of,' Marigold chimed.

'So, we're going to meet with someone who makes giant traps!' Morris shouted loudly so that Bam could hear.

'Guess again!' she called back to them, and they sank back into their hushed tones.

'Bam doesn't like killing things,' Marigold reminded him.

'She doesn't mind when Mack kills mice!' Morris said, throwing up his hands.

'To be fair, Mack very rarely kills mice. He plays with them and chases them away.' Marigold shrugged.

'And, besides, cats catching mice is the natural order of things. Humans killing mice with nasty traps and poisons isn't very fair on the poor little mites,' Bam said to them as she rounded a corner, and the children quickened their pace to catch up before they lost her entirely.

'So if Mack is the best way Bam can think of to get rid of mice . . .' Morris turned to look at Marigold with a glint in his eye.

'But Mack isn't able to get rid of this many mice alone . . .' Marigold grinned at him.

'Then he'll need a little bit of help, won't he?' Bam said, stopping dead in her tracks and spinning round with a triumphant flourish of her fur coat. Behind her was a sign that said: **BATTERSEA DOGS AND CATS HOME**

'Oh, my goodness!' Marigold cried.

'Bam, are you for real?' Morris said as he danced for joy in a circle round his aunt.

'Of course I'm "for real",' she said, her fingers air-quoting. 'I'm also very serious about this cat-and-mouse business. We *have* a home with lots of lovely mice and these cats *need* a home with lots of lovely mice. So, shall we go and look at some potential theatre moggies?' Marigold and Morris hugged each other and then they both hugged Bam before they headed inside together.

'There are so many, Marigold! How will we ever choose?' Inside the home, there were more cats than Marigold and Morris could ever have imagined. Morris was awfully excited, but it made Marigold a little sad to think that so many cats had been left without laps to curl up on. The smell of disinfectant filled the air and slightly stung their nostrils. It reminded them all of the times they'd had to take Mack to the vet. The sound of meowing made Morris's heart leap and he sped off, peering in through the first glass door in a row that seemed to go on forever. There were other people milling about, looking for feline additions to their families. There were a few young children pouting and blubbing as their parents pulled them away from mewing kittens.

'We aren't here for just any moggies, Morris. We're here for *theatre* cats. Not just any cat can be a theatre cat, in the same way that not just any person can be a theatre person.'

'What makes a person a theatre person?' Morris asked, scratching his head.

'Firstly, you'd have to be OK with loud noises. Lots of shows have sound effects and even pyrotechnics that give off a great big bang,' Bam said. 'You can't be easily spooked.'

'You'd also have to be OK with talking to lots of people every day, and happy to work with children and animals,' Marigold explained.

'And it's a very active job,' Bam said. 'You need a lot of energy and you need to be fit enough to rush about here, there and everywhere.'

'I'm all those things!' Morris shouted, and was promptly shushed by one of the workers who wore a dark blue uniform that made them look like a nurse in a hospital.

'Of course you are. You grew up in a theatre, so you've had a big head start.'

'So, we're looking for a young, energetic cat that's OK with loud noises, people, children and other cats.' Marigold listed them on her fingers. 'Isn't that quite a tall order?'

'Maybe.' Bam shrugged. 'But we might be lucky! Come on. They're all waiting!'

It seemed it wouldn't be a tall order at all. There were so many cats of many different kinds. Younger kittens zoomed around in circles in their enclosures. Older cats snoozed in corners on blankets. Some cats shied away from them as they walked past and others stuck their little pink noses up against the glass to get a better look.

'How will we ever choose?' Marigold looked about the room and took in just how many cats there were staring back at her — each of them desperately willing her to pick them with their big sparkling eyes, their twitching wet noses and, some of them, their piercing meows.

'You'll know when you know.'

'How about this one?' said Morris, pointing to a grey long-haired cat with a scowl on his little face. As the tip of Morris's finger touched the glass, the cat hissed with such ferocity that Morris yelped and stumbled backwards into Marigold. 'Never mind the mice! This cat would scare all the people away!'

'Maybe one a little more docile?' Bam steered Morris by

the shoulders to the other side of the room, away from the hostile moggy that was still hissing at them as they walked away. As they wandered round the room, Marigold locked eyes with an all-black cat that seemed to be watching her. The cat was big and puffed out its chest when Marigold paid it attention. She noticed that it stood with its front paws pulled neatly together, almost as if it was standing in a ballerina's first position. It had a sad face with almost human features, and Marigold felt desperate to give it a stroke and a cuddle. She tilted her head to the side and the cat did the same. She tilted her head to the other side and the cat followed. Marigold opened her mouth to suggest they check out this curious cat, but Morris called out.

'What about this one? It looks a bit like Mack!' Morris gestured towards a ginger cat that raised its head and yawned as they approached. It pushed itself to standing but could only manage to hobble towards them, and it wasn't until it got closer to them that they realized it was perhaps not the youngest cat Morris could have picked.

'Yeah, if Mack was a hundred years old!' Marigold scoffed, but still made kissing noises to entice him closer.

'Hey, now!' Bam said, giving Marigold a playful shove out of the way to bend towards the glass and get a closer look. 'Older people . . . I mean . . . older *cats* . . . need a little love too.'

'Of course they do.' Marigold smiled, putting a hand on

her aunt's shoulder. 'But I doubt this one has the energy required to chase lots of mice around, let alone catch them.'

'Yes, I suppose you're right.' Bam sighed, but suddenly their hunt for mouse-catchers was interrupted by a low and long howl. 'What is that awful racket?'

'Is that a dog or a cat?' Morris asked, already hunting for where the sound was coming from.

'It's definitely a cat, but I've never heard anything quite like it,' said Bam.

'Where is it coming from?' Marigold went and checked along the left side of the room and Morris checked the right.

'Over here!' Morris beckoned from the furthest end of the room. 'Look!' Marigold and Bam quickly joined Morris, who was on his hands and knees in front of the last enclosure on the bottom row. The other people there either couldn't hear the yowling cat or were choosing to ignore it, but Morris was hypnotized. The cat was white with a black tuft of fur on his chest and little black paws.

'He looks like he's wearing tap shoes!' Morris giggled. He didn't seem very old, and began to walk in excited circles when he saw he had company. The long drawn-out howls ceased and he started to let out little high-pitched mews.

'Oh, Brilliant Aunt Maude . . .' Morris put his hand flat against the glass, to which the cat responded by putting his paw against the other side of the glass right in the centre of Morris's palm.

'I told you, kid. You'll know when you know.'

'I think I know,' Morris said, gazing at the cat with glistening eyes. Bam's throat began to close up at the sight of her favourite little boy finding a best friend, so she averted her gaze and looked at Marigold who was smiling down at her little brother.

'He's called Maestro.' Marigold pointed to the sign on the glass. 'He's three years old, happy to live with other cats and will make a lot of noise until he's cuddled.'

'He's perfect! Bam . . . what do you think?' Morris looked up at his aunt from his crouched position on the floor, his big round eyes beginning to well up.

Just as they were about to brim over, Bam smiled. 'I think Maestro would make a perfect addition to our family.'

'Oh, Bam! Thank you! Thank you! Thank you!' Morris jumped up and threw his arms round Brilliant Aunt Maude. She gave the top of his head a big kiss.

'So that just leaves you now, Marigold. Have you found a companion you'd like to take home yet?'

'What?' Marigold gasped.

'You didn't think we were just here to pick out a cat for Morris, did you?' Bam asked, and Marigold shrugged and shuffled her shoes. 'You silly goose!' Bam stroked Marigold's perfectly sleek hair and fought the urge to ruffle it. 'Mack definitely needs a couple of feline friends to make sure our theatre is rodent-free by opening night. Go and find your

165

moggy.' Bam shooed her away and so Marigold quickly hurried down the corridor of cats to find that beautiful all-black cat who had looked at her in such a funny way. Brilliant Aunt Maude had said 'When you know, you'll know', and Marigold was certain that she knew. That cat was meant for her. But where was it? She was sure it had been just across from the angry grey cat, that still hissed as she neared it, but directly opposite was a tabby cat whose eyes were slightly crossed. Just as she was starting to panic that someone had offered to take her cat home in the brief time she'd been away, she heard a tap-tap-tapping. Her head whipped round to her right and – just a little bit further along than she had first thought – was her cat.

'Hello, there. I thought I'd lost you . . . Morticia!'

'Morticia, eh? Is this your cat?' asked Bam, joining her.

'I'd like her to be. Female, OK to live with children . . . oh, no . . . Bam, she doesn't like fireworks. She'd never be OK with all the pyrotechnics on stage.' Marigold couldn't help it. Her bottom lip began to wobble and a tear spilt over and rolled down her cheek. She quickly wiped it away with the back of her hand before her aunt or her brother saw. Bam crouched down next to Marigold, even though it took her a little while and her bones creaked as she did so, but she needed to get a good look in Marigold's eyes.

'Are you certain this is your cat, Marigold?' Marigold's big golden eyes shone and she didn't need to say a word. Bam had made up her mind. 'Well, in that case, the Pebble Theatre is now a pyro-free zone, as far as I'm concerned. As long as that doesn't mess up anything in your fabulous show?' Marigold leapt at Brilliant Aunt Maude, sending her backwards on to her bottom. She buried her head into the faux-fur coat and let it soak up her tears. It took her a few moments to catch her breath before she could sob, 'Thank you.'

# 21

## The Empty Shelves

The research trip and the new additions to their theatre family still hadn't given Marigold the inspiration she needed. It seemed to be hiding from her and no amount of searching could uncover it. She'd barely written anything for the play at all apart from the opening scenes, which still didn't feel quite right, and panic had begun to set in. How could she possibly turn the Fossil sisters' journal into a play? How could she pretend to know three people she'd never actually met, let alone write a play all about their lives? And what if everyone hated it when she did finally finish it so the Pebble Theatre had to be sold and it was all her fault? A lot of thoughts were whizzing round her brain and she didn't know how to slow any of them down.

'How's it going, Shakespeare?' Lydia said after politely rapping on the door, and Marigold groaned in response. Lydia entered to see Marigold with her forehead pressed against the desk and her eyes shut tight as she clicked the end of her pen repeatedly. Marigold groaned again. 'Not going so well, eh? Is there anything I can do to help?' Lydia set down a glass of strawberry-and-banana smoothie on the desk next to Marigold's notebook. 'I thought all the vitamins might get those creative juices flowing!' Lydia couldn't help but glance down and see that the page was empty.

'Can you write the play instead?' Marigold lifted her head to show Lydia her pleading eyes.

'Is it still writer's block?'

'Something like that.' Marigold shrugged.

'OK. I'm going to tell Bam enough is enough. This is far too much pressure to put on the shoulders of someone so young.' Lydia stood and took a step towards the door but Marigold jumped up and beat her to it, flinging herself at the door and slamming it closed.

'No! I can do it! I can do it!' Marigold cried.

'Then what's going on?' Lydia sat in Marigold's seat at the desk and, when Marigold trudged towards her with dragging feet, Lydia took both of her hands and stroked her palms with her thumbs. This was something she used to do when

Marigold was having a tantrum when she was little and needed to be calmed down.

'I know I can do it. I'm just . . .' Marigold took a long and deep breath. 'I'm just scared of what happens afterwards.'

'What do you mean? After what?'

'After we put on the play.' Marigold began to pace back and forth. 'What if everyone hates it and we have to sell the theatre anyway? What if this is the start *and* the end of my career as a writer? What if –'

'You need to go and have a chat with Dawson,' Lydia blurted out.

'Dawson? Why? What does Dawson have to do with anything?' Marigold's cheeks instantly flushed at the mere mention of his name.

'You just . . . do. Trust me. I'll go and give him a heads-up now, but before the day is out you need to go and listen to what he has to say.'

'Are you sure he actually speaks when he's not on stage? I've never heard *Dawson* speak, I've only ever heard the *characters* speak.' Dawson's dressing room was maybe the only dressing room Marigold had never been in. It was his sacred space to get into character before every show. No one other than Dante was allowed in it.

Lydia rolled her eyes. 'He definitely speaks, but only when he feels like what he says will make a difference. I'm sure this will be one of those moments.'

Marigold couldn't possibly imagine that anything a serious and almost-silent middle-aged actor said would make any difference to her, but when she thought about her very full head and her very blank notebook, and how she couldn't find a way to empty one into the other, she knew she had to give it a try. She was also a little excited about having an actual conversation with someone who'd barely said two words to her in her whole life. Marigold closed her notebook, accepting defeat for the afternoon, and said, 'OK. I'll go and speak to him after lunch.'

While Cora and Layton, Kitty and Claudia, and Theodore always kept their dressing room doors open, Dawson's was always firmly closed. However, on this one occasion, Marigold had permission to visit, though she had no idea how Dawson was going to help her with her writer's block. She stood outside for at least ten minutes before building up the courage to knock three times, very gently. She was hoping there would be no answer and she'd have an excuse to run away, but the door opened almost immediately and she was greeted with Dante's smiling face.

'Marigold, my darling girl! Come in! Come in! I've just brewed some tea. Would you like some?'

Marigold would have loved some but that would have meant staying until she'd drunk it all so she shook her head politely and said, 'No, thank you.'

'Well, sit down, anyway.' Dante gestured to the armchair

in the corner and closed the door behind Marigold. Dawson was sitting at the dressing-room mirror, putting on his stage make-up even though there was no performance that evening.

'Dawson, darling. Let's not ignore our company.'

Dawson put down his brush and looked at Marigold through the mirror. 'How much do you know?' His voice was almost a whisper.

'Kn-know?' Marigold stammered. She cleared her dry throat.

'What have Lydia and Maude told you?' Dante asked gently as he poured hot water from the kettle into his blue mug.

'About what?' Marigold looked at them both. Dante's face was always smiling and warm while Dawson very rarely smiled and seemed to be all sharp edges and angles.

'The empty case,' Dawson said with his eyes closed tight, as if it pained him to speak of it.

'The . . . empty case?'

'I think you'll need to start from the beginning, my love,' Dante said to Dawson, stirring his tea. It was then that Dante moved to sit cross-legged on the floor and revealed an ornate wooden cabinet behind him. It had a glass front and sides, which let Marigold see that all the shelves were empty.

'Dim the lights,' Dawson said.

'Must we, really?' Dante groaned, having just sat down.

'The only way I can tell the story is to perform it.'

'All right, sweetheart.' Dante reached up and rolled the dimmer switch with the tips of his fingers.

Dawson stood abruptly and faced away from Marigold. He rolled his R's and then made strange noises with his voice that made him sound like a police siren. Then he turned to Marigold, his eyes closed, and began . . .

'Once upon a time, I was a small boy who was destined for the stage. There was nothing I loved more than telling stories to my parents and acting out my favourite scenes from my favourite plays and movies.'

Marigold couldn't believe how quickly Dawson could transform himself. He was still Dawson, but at the same time he wasn't. He was confident and full of life and could look her in the eye, when only moments ago he wouldn't even turn away from the mirror to look at her properly.

'Everyone told me I'd win awards one day. That I'd be a star. The best of the best. Like Laurence Olivier or John Gielgud. No one had a doubt in their mind. No one . . . except me.' Dawson hung his head. 'I knew I was talented. I knew I had the potential to go far. I knew all this and yet, every time I stepped on to the stage, my knees began to knock, my head began to spin, my tongue would tie itself in knots and all I could think was that everyone was looking at me.' Something in the pit of Marigold's stomach tightened. 'What if I forgot my lines? What if I picked up the wrong prop? What if I fell over? What if I got something wrong and everyone laughed when they weren't meant to laugh? What if they laughed *at* me and not *with* me? What if everyone hated my performance? What if? What if? What if?'

Marigold hadn't realized she was getting upset until a tear spilt over on to her cheek, and she quickly wiped it away with the back of her hand. She was so sucked into Dawson's story because he was describing exactly how she felt.

'I drove myself mad with all the wondering until I came to a grinding halt.' Dante bowed his head and sipped his tea quietly, as if he'd heard this story a thousand times and yet it was still never easy to hear. 'When I was younger, my father made me that cabinet in the corner. "For all the awards you'll win some day," he'd said. He believed in me more than I ever did and for that reason the case has stayed empty. I never believed in myself and I let all my worst fears control my life.'

'But . . . but . . . you've performed here, for years! You're still doing what you love!' Marigold protested.

'I have! You're right! But that's only because your Brilliant Aunt Maude did me a great kindness in letting me perform here. She promised me small and quiet audiences to build up my courage and I've been very lucky that they have stayed small and quiet ever since I arrived. But . . . but that doesn't have to be you, Marigold. Don't let your fears and worries take over.' Dawson knelt down on one knee in front of Marigold and took the hand that wasn't clutching her notebook. As he spoke he traced its wrinkles with his fingertip, as if he were about to read her fortune. 'You have a great, big, beautiful future full of fulfilled wishes and dreams come true. Never let the clouds of "what if" and "could be" stop you from finding out what your life is meant to look like. People regret the chances they *didn't* take in life. Very rarely do they regret the chances they did. Constantly wondering what could have been is no way to spend a life. Take chances and make mistakes. Your shelves should collect awards, not dust.' Finally, Dawson gave Marigold a kiss on her forehead then looked at her through his weary grey eyes. 'Be a little less Dawson Sanders and a little more . . . Marigold Pebble.'

Dawson had given Marigold an awful lot to think about. At first, Dawson's story had made her feel awfully strange. She was sad for Dawson and the life he'd missed out on. This weighed heavy on her heart, but she also felt a huge burden had been lifted from her mind. Life and all its chances were there for the taking. She raced out of Dawson's dressing room, after planting a giant kiss on his cheek that left him quite taken aback, but he'd smiled warmly and sent her on her way. Her fingers were tingling, almost itching for her pen. It was as if Dawson had broken a dam in her brain and all these words seemed to be pouring forth. She knew if she didn't get to her notebook soon, they'd tumble out of her brain and she'd have nothing in which to catch them. She couldn't risk losing them after she'd spent so long searching for them! She burst into her writing room, threw open her notebook and began to write – and she didn't stop writing for hours.

# 22

# Rain, Rain, Go Away!

Morris was on stage and taking his role as head choreographer very seriously.

'Bourrée, échappé and pirouette!' Morris sang, demonstrating each movement with ease as Kitty and Claudia followed along behind him, their golden sequinned leotards sparkling in the theatre's bright working lights – the special lights they used specifically for rehearsals.

'Morris, how have you learnt all this?' Kitty said breathlessly, and Morris puffed out his chest with pride.

'Lady at the library let me watch some videos on the computer there, and I borrowed some books with pictures of all the different types of moves so I could practise in my room. I'm not sure I'm getting any of them exactly right, though. It's hard when there's no one to teach you,' he said, expertly pirouetting once more.

'Well, you're doing marvellously for someone who's never had a lesson.' Kitty applauded him and he bowed elegantly.

'We will teach you as much as we know, but I think you should chat to Lydia about getting some proper training!' Claudia said, and they both grinned excitedly.

'Oh, I would love that!' Morris's heart bounced and then promptly sank. 'But . . . I think Lydia and Bam have enough to worry about right now. Maybe when the theatre has officially been saved I can . . .' Morris trailed off as something wet landed on the tip of his nose from above. Then again. Then again and again and again until it was raining on stage.

'What's going on?' Morris wiped his nose with his sleeve.

'Oh no . . . !' Claudia said, pointing up to the fly floor, a space above the stage where the crew could change the set from one scene to another by pulling ropes and lifting it up, up and out of the way.

'Look out below!' someone called from up above, and suddenly the rain got so heavy you could hear it pitter-patter against the stage. It rained harder and harder until the droplets thundered down, soaking absolutely everything.

'Is this a new special effect?' Morris yelled over the noise of the droplets hitting the stage, covering his head.

'I wish it was, but I didn't sign up for this!' Bam shrieked, rushing in from the auditorium, pulling her fur coat round her with one hand and fishing in her handbag for an umbrella with the other. She found it but Kitty and Claudia shrieked, 'NO!' in unison.

'You can't put an umbrella up!' Kitty said.

'Disastrous bad luck!' Claudia agreed.

'Do you really think my luck could get any worse?' Bam said as she ignored them both. She clicked a button and her umbrella shot up, fanning out above her head.

'Roof's caved in, Maude!' cried the voice from the top of the theatre. Everyone looked up and squinted to see there were five orbs of the grey sky looming overhead.

'Yes, I can see that, Theo! Thank you! Five giant holes,' Bam groaned, taking off her glasses and wiping them on her coat. 'Five holes that need to be fixed by opening night unless Marigold's willing to dump her play and we do *Singin' in the Rain* instead.'

'We could risk it? It might not rain on the night?' Morris said, tucking himself under Bam's arm to escape the rain.

'Maybe not . . .' She thought for a moment and then kicked into action. 'Mops! We need mops, buckets and towels!' Bam raced into the wings and Morris followed.

'Rehearsal's cancelled until further notice, ladies!' he yelled back to Kitty and Claudia, but they were already scuttling into the wings back to their dressing room to dry off.

Bam and Morris were almost at the stage door to ask Petunia to make a few calls, when Marigold rushed down the stairs and almost barrelled into them.

'My goodness, Marigold! Whatever is the matter?!' Marigold was so out of breath that she wasn't able to answer Bam. Instead she just thrust at her a handful of pages torn out of her notebook that were so covered in scrawled handwriting they looked more black than white. 'Is this what I think it is?'

'It's the first act!' Marigold gasped for air in between words. Bam pushed her glasses up her nose and gave the pages a quick scan. She glanced at the empty header.

'No title?'

'No title yet, but at least I've actually made a start!' Marigold wouldn't let the lack of a title weigh down her spirits on such a triumphant day.

'Looks like it's all coming along nicely. Go and get a cup of tea and keep going! You've managed to catch that inspiration and hold it down for long enough to get started!' Marigold took her pages and began to run upstairs. 'Wait!' Bam called after her. 'I'm going to need a copy of those . . .'

'Luvvies and Jellicles,' Bam addressed the entirety of the Pebble Theatre. They had all gathered in the seats of the auditorium as it was still drizzling slightly on stage. The buckets were almost overflowing and would need to be emptied and replaced very soon. Everyone was there, hanging on Bam's every word. Everyone, that is, except Marigold. 'We have the entire first act of Marigold's marvellous play! She's back at her writing desk with a pot of tea and a head full of ideas, but I thought we'd get a head start on at least reading some of it through. Marigold has also kindly given me a list of characters so I can start dishing out roles.'

'Who do you think will be playing Posy?' Morris whispered out of the corner of his mouth to Mabel.

'I bet Kitty and Claudia will play two of the sisters. Probably Pauline and Posy,' Mabel whispered back behind her curtain of hair.

'That would be awfully clever considering they actually are sisters. Trouble is, they are awfully . . .' He trailed off, desperately trying to find the right words.

'Maybe just a little . . .' Mabel attempted.

'Youthfully challenged?' Morris suggested and Mabel snort-laughed, which earned her a slightly searing look from Lydia.

'Very kindly put, Morris.' She giggled in spite of Lydia's disapproving shake of the head.

'Who would play Petrova?' Morris looked around the ragtag group of actors.

'You know,' Mabel said, sitting up in her seat, looking at the wrinkled faces of her Pebble Theatre family. 'I hadn't actually noticed just how old everyone is.'

'Me neither. I'm starting to worry a little that this . . .'

'This might be a disaster.' Mabel and Morris exchanged a fretful sideways look.

'Mabel and Morris.' Bam raised her voice. 'Would you come and join me for a moment?' The two Pebble children looked at each other and gulped. They hadn't heard a thing Bam had said while they were chatting to each other. Nervous that they'd missed something important, they shuffled out from their row and made baby steps towards Brilliant Aunt Maude.

'Hurry now! That's it!' Bam placed her hands on their shoulders and sandwiched herself between them. Her red claws felt dangerously close to their faces so neither of them moved for fear of being accidentally scratched.

'Dearest members of the Pebble clan. In my opinion, our beloved theatre is home to the world's greatest talent.' Bam looked out at her family and felt her heart swell with pride. 'However, it's time that we introduced some fresh meat and new blood. Talent that the world has never seen.' Mabel and Morris sneaked yet another glance at each other, wondering where Bam was going with this, and why they were both standing facing the hopeful eyes and eager smiles of their Pebble family. 'So, without further ado, may I present Mabel and Morris Pebble, or should I say . . . Petrova and Posy Fossil!' Everyone burst into applause and some even rose to their feet. However, Lydia's face sank into her palms and Mabel and Morris whipped round to face Aunt Maude, who for a brief moment had become not-so-brilliant.

'WHAT?!' they shouted.

'*Whaaaat?*' Bam sang, with a smile playing at the corners of her mouth. 'I thought you'd be pleased! Especially you, Morris! You idolize Posy so much!'

'Yes, but I can't *be* her!' Morris felt his cheeks grow warm. Bam crouched down to his eye level and lowered her voice while the audience talked among themselves. Dante leant over two rows to shake Mabel's hand. Despite being absolutely mortified, she still took his hand and smiled gratefully, although Dante didn't see it as her hair now covered her whole face.

'Morris, you'd be so wasted behind the scenes! This way, you'd get to dance just like her. In front of an audience. Your dancing debut . . .'

Morris had been staring at his feet but now that he glanced up at his aunt he could see her eyes were glistening – and it wasn't because of the dust from all the set renovations. He could tell.

'But he's a boy!' Mabel hissed.

'I'm well aware of that, Mabel, but in the world of theatre when has that ever mattered?' Bam actually rolled her eyes at Mabel. Mabel rolled her eyes back and Morris laughed in spite of himself.

'I can't play Posy, Bam. All the kids at school will . . .'

'Will what? Laugh?'

Morris nodded solemnly.

Bam knelt by his side. 'Children can be cruel, my dear. But this isn't about them. Do you want to play Posy?'

His lowered gaze finally lifted to meet his aunt's. 'People will say mean things,' Morris whispered, a hot tear spilling over. He sniffled quietly.

'Let them. It's only because they don't understand, and they may never understand, but . . . turn around.' Morris turned to look at everyone. 'Do you think any of them had an easy time of it growing up? Contortionist twins, a tattooed stuntman with two left feet, an actor and a musician with the hots for each other . . . We've all had our fair share of bullies, but do you know what got us through? Each other. This theatre has always been a place of acceptance, no matter who you are or what you've been through. Some people outside these walls might not understand. But *we* do.' Morris wiped his eyes and nodded so hard his head almost came off his shoulders.

'I'll do it!' he shouted, and everyone cheered.

Bam beamed. 'Besides, girls weren't allowed on stage back in the olden days and so all the boys wore dresses and make-up. It'll be utterly marvellous!'

'I'm a bit scared.' He giggled nervously.

'You'd be mad not to be. That's theatre, darling.' Bam kissed him on both cheeks, leaving big red lipstick marks behind.

'You did kind of spring this on us, Bam!' Mabel said.

'People often give you a quicker answer under a little bit of pressure.' Bam shrugged.

'Well, this is a *lot* of pressure!' Mabel folded her arms across her chest and shook her hair out of her face just enough so that Bam could see one glaring eye.

'You fancy giving it a go though, don't you . . .' Bam found Mabel's nose in among her hair and gave it a playful prod with the tip of her nail.

'I'm not an actress!' Mabel threw up her hands, and by accident some of her hair, in despair.

'You could have fooled me!' Bam threw back her head and laughed, her silver curls bobbing as she bellowed. 'I've seen you a million times over get out of going to bed early or doing chores by pouting or giving Lydia crocodile tears, so don't you fib to me, Mabel Pebble. Besides, with Morris here playing Posy, it wouldn't be right that you weren't up there with him!' Mabel glanced at her little brother, who gave her his largest puppy-dog eyes, and she softened just a smidgen.

'Why does Marigold get out of doing this?' she huffed.

'She doesn't. Who do you think I want to play Pauline?' Bam said, laughing and hugging Mabel and Morris to her as if that was the end of the discussion.

'No!' said Lydia, who until now had been lost for words. 'No, no, no. Aunt Maude, you are brilliant in so many ways but this is not one of them. Mabel's already said it – too much pressure!'

'No pressure, no diamonds!' Bam gestured to Mabel and

Morris as if they were the precious gems she spoke of. 'Most people would jump at the opportunity to perform on a London stage, and our three will be able to say they did it before they'd even turned thirteen!'

'But what about when the children go back to school?'

'Do they have to go back to school?'

'Bam . . .' Lydia said in a warning tone the children knew only too well.

'All right, all right. I'll have to hire some more young actors to rehearse with us at the same time so they can alternate when we open. Like the big shows do in the West End. Simple!' Bam shrugged.

'Maude . . .' Lydia sighed, knowing there was very little she could ever say that would lure her aunt away from an idea once it had lodged itself inside her brain. 'I just think there are other ways of saving this theatre.'

A huge crash from the back of the auditorium made everyone jump violently, including Layton. He had seized the opportunity to catch forty winks in his seat during the Pebble family's private discussion. He was jolted awake and began to applaud and shout 'Bravo'. Cora laughed and gave him a kiss on the cheek, taking no notice of the bright pink vision that was floating up the aisle towards them. Trixabellina had pushed through the doors so violently that they'd jammed open behind her, letting in a dreadful cold gust of wind that made everyone shiver in their seats.

'You're right. There are better ways to save this theatre, Liesel.'

'It's Lydia, actually . . .'

'It seems that very little progress has been made since my last visit. Such a shame.' Trixabellina pulled her glasses down her nose and peered disdainfully at the almost-overflowing buckets on the stage, the half-finished dripping set and the cast of misfits gathered in the stalls, some with towels wrapped round their heads still drying off.

'No shame here,' Bam said, her shoulders visibly stiffening and her nose rising into the air. 'We're very proud of our theatre and our *big* plans to save it.'

'Plans? What plans?' A smile started to appear at the edges of Trixabellina's sharply lined and perfectly plump lips. 'I hear you have a child writing a show for you that your band of ragtag theatre veterans are to perform!' She couldn't help herself and let out a high-pitched trill of a laugh that sounded more like a soprano singing a delicate aria than laughter. 'Besides that, you've also got holes in your roof and from what I hear there are rats crawling out of every nook and cranny. Hardly a foolproof plan now, is it?'

'How could you possibly know about the rain and the mice?' Lydia put her arm round Mabel and held on to her tightly. Mabel couldn't tell if it was for her sake or Lydia's. Trixabellina von Hustle the Third smoothed down her pink jacket.

'I have my sources . . .'

'Now you just wait a minute –' Bam began, but was cut off by the auditorium being plunged into darkness. However, a spotlight remained on stage.

'*Pssst! Pssst!*' It was Marigold, desperately calling out to Mabel and Morris from the wings as she pushed the lever round and round to make the curtains close. Her brother and sister hopped, skipped and jumped on to the stage and disappeared behind the curtain.

'What's going on?!' Mabel hissed, helping to operate the lever.

'Take these.' Marigold handed them a few pieces of paper that were stapled along the left edge. Printed on them was the first scene of the show. 'I was just typing up the first scene on Petunia's computer when we heard Trixabellina von Kerfuffle show up over the tannoy system! Morris, you'll be –'

'Posy! Got it!'

'And, Mabel, you are –'

'Petrova! And you –'

'Will be Pauline, I know. I heard.' Marigold rolled her eyes but smiled nonetheless. 'Let's show that fluorescent meanie who's got plans!' Marigold fumbled to find the parting in the curtains and, when she did, she stumbled through, tripping over the hem. She cleared her throat loudly but everyone's eyes were already on her. She was thankful she knew where the switch for the auditorium lights was, because she couldn't see anyone at all. She needed to pretend no one was there to get through the next few minutes.

'Once upon a time,' Marigold read from the papers that were trembling between her fingers, 'there were three sisters. Pauline . . .' She looked up and smiled. 'Petrova . . .' Mabel appeared by her side right on cue. 'And Posy.' Morris came through the curtain, and once in his spot on the other side of Marigold he twirled in a neat pirouette, finishing with a cheeky grin that earned him a light smattering of applause from their small audience. Marigold couldn't hide her smile. *Maybe this will be a little bit fun after all*, she thought.

'They were orphans and had been rescued by their brave great-uncle Matthew, whom they liked to call Gum. First came Pauline. Gum was on his travels when his ship hit an iceberg and all the passengers had to cram into lifeboats.' Marigold had scribbled *Climb into my lifeboat!* on Mabel's and Morris's scripts, so they did exactly that, pretending to clamber aboard with Marigold at the helm.

'But in the night, one of the boats sank and, by the time Gum's boat had got there, everyone had drowned . . .' The audience gasped right on cue while Morris ducked down behind his sisters to pull off his jumper and roll it up into a little oblong. 'Except for . . . a baby!' Morris lifted his jumper into the air as if he were in the opening scene of *The Lion King* and again everyone cheered.

'Great-uncle Matthew rescued the baby, brought her home

and named her Pauline.' Marigold curtseyed. 'However, it wasn't very long until Gum brought home a sister for her to play with. While in hospital, Great-uncle Matthew made friends with a man from Russia. His wife had died and he was very ill too. He did not know what would happen to his daughter. Great-uncle Matthew came to the rescue once again and Petrova became one of the family.' Mabel leapt into centre stage, threw all her hair behind her shoulders and blew a kiss to the audience. Marigold was so shocked she forgot to carry on reading. She was sure it had been years since she'd seen her sister's whole face all at once. Even Morris was staring.

'Bravo!' Bam cried.

'And then there was Posy, the daughter of a dancer whose father had died and whose mother could not look after her any longer. She arrived at Great-uncle Matthew's house with nothing but a pair of ballet shoes to her name, a sure sign that dancing was in her blood.' Morris had begun to spin on just one foot, kicking out his other leg, spinning himself round and round. Just when Marigold thought he would get dizzy and stop, he carried on – and on. The crowd began to go wild and egg him on, chanting, '*Posy! Posy! Posy!*'

Finally Morris finished, with a flourish of his hands and the biggest grin Marigold had ever seen on his face. When the cheers of the crowd had died down, Marigold continued with her last little bit.

'They all lived in a house on Cromwell Road, where they were looked after by Sylvia, whom they called Garnie. She was the closest thing they had to a mother and they loved her as such.' Marigold couldn't help but squint through the darkness in the auditorium to Lydia, who she hoped was listening closely. 'Even though they were fragments from different families from different corners of the world, they fit together perfectly. They might have been a little lopsided, a bit mismatched and frayed around the edges, but they were a family nonetheless. And families stick together, no matter what.' Marigold felt her breath catch in her throat and so, even though it wasn't Morris's line, he carried on for his sister.

'Even when your feet are tired . . .' He linked arms with Marigold on her left.

'Even when the sky is dark . . .' Mabel linked arms with Marigold on her right and nudged her to say the last few lines of her script.

'. . . and you've got nothing left to say, families always pull each other close and move forward, together.' There was silence in the theatre, save for a little sniffle coming from Lydia's direction. Suddenly, someone was clapping from the back of the stalls. When that person rose to their feet in a well-deserved standing ovation, they caught some of the light from the stage and the Pebble children could see that it was Theodore, tears glistening on his cheeks. One by one,

Petunia, Kitty, Claudia, Layton, Cora, Dante and even Dawson were on their feet, clapping, cheering, whooping and whistling – who knew better than this ragtag bunch what it was to be a family? Bam and Lydia hugged each other tight, unable to catch their breath through their proud tears. Bam thought of the perfect final words to say to the woman in pink before she kicked her out of the theatre, but she turned just in time to see a pink heel disappear out of the auditorium doors as they swung firmly shut behind Trixabellina.

# 23

## The Power of the Internet

The performance Marigold, Mabel and Morris had hurriedly put together on the spot ignited a spark inside the theatre that day. There hadn't been a dry eye in the house. Everyone had been moved beyond words. The Pebbles hugged each other close after Trixabellina had scurried away. One by one the family made their way on to the stage to join the huddle. It was at this moment they all realized that this might just be possible. The theatre *could* be saved if they all came together. The fire in everyone's heart began to spread and, with only three weeks to go, they sprang into action. The sets were built and painted in record time. Costumes were recycled from old ones found in the storage cupboard (after they'd been given a thorough clean and all the sleeves and pockets had been checked for mice and moths). Morris found an old pair of ballet shoes in a box at the back of the highest shelf. When no one was looking, he took the box up to their room and tried them on and, just like Cinderella, they fit him almost magically. Most importantly, Marigold finally finished the script.

'*The End!*' she shrieked, not realizing it was almost two o'clock in the morning. Waving not one but two notebooks, she barrelled down the corridor and scrambled up the stairs to Bam and Lydia.

'*BAM! LYDIA! I'VE DONE IT! I'VE DONE IT!*' As she approached Bam's bedroom, the door burst open and out came Bam, with her hair up in rollers, her eye mask still pulled down over her eyes and both her slippers in her hands.

'*Step away from my Pebbles!*' she yelled, brandishing a hairbrush she'd snatched up from her bedside table. Mabel and Morris's door opened and their sleepy faces appeared out of the darkness of their room.

'What's going on?' Morris yawned, not opening his eyes. Marigold reached up and pulled Bam's eye mask up so she could see.

'Is everyone OK?' Lydia scurried up the corridor from behind them, tying her grey dressing gown round her.

'Act one . . .' Marigold held out one notebook to Lydia. 'And act two,' she said, holding out the other to Bam.

'It's finished?' Bam said, now wide awake and alert. She took the notebook and flipped right to the final page to see the words *The End* smiling back at her.

'It's finished,' Marigold confirmed. Lydia began to read the first act and instantly became emotional.

'Oh, Marigold,' she whispered. Bam joined her and began to read over her shoulder, coughing every now and then to disguise a little sob. Now that the books were out of her hands, Marigold burst into tears on the spot and no amount of hugging could staunch the flow. She felt like she'd crossed the finish line of a hundred back-to-back marathons. Never before had she completed a task quite so huge, which meant she wasn't prepared to feel quite as proud of herself as she did. Marigold also wasn't prepared for as many people to feel equally proud of her.

'Whatever is the matter?' Bam dropped to her knees and pulled Marigold into a bear hug. 'You should be thrilled! It's absolutely perfect.'

'I – I . . . I a-am thrilled.' Marigold broke into more sobs and sniffles. When she'd finally composed herself a little, she added, 'I'm just also relieved. I can't believe I did it.'

'Well, believe it, madam! You finished your very own show, which is called . . .' Bam prompted.

'I'm sorry, Bam. I just can't think of a title yet. Maybe when you read it, you'll be able to work something out?'

'It's all right! It'll come to you, dear! However, the hard

work doesn't end there. Once we get actors reading it and you hear lines said out loud, you might want to change things.'

'I think I might need a hot chocolate first . . .'

'Marigold, you read my mind! Late-night . . . well . . . early-morning hot chocolates all round. This is a special occasion!'

The family went to the kitchen and Lydia made proper hot chocolate with real chocolate and milk. Bam made a toast to Marigold and all her hard work and Marigold made everyone laugh by bursting into tears again.

Once their drinks were finished, they all went back to bed. Rehearsals started the following morning on the stage, underneath a shabbily patched roof.


'We have three weeks until opening night!' Bam declared to the cast and crew on their first official day of rehearsing Marigold's script.

'*Three weeks?!* Is that all?' Lydia squeaked, not realizing how much of the summer holidays had already passed.

'That's barely even enough time to find my character, let alone learn the lines and the staging,' Dawson muttered.

'What about the set?!' shouted Cora.

'And the props!' groaned Lydia.

'And the stunts?!' squawked Theodore.

'And the dancing?!' shrieked Kitty, Claudia and Morris.

'And the illusions?!' called Dante and Mabel.

'And all the lines?!' cried Layton.

'Settle down! Settle down!' Bam said with a smile, hoping her positivity was infectious, as it so often was. 'Where's our enthusiasm? Where's our team spirit, eh?'

'I'm sorry, Bam,' said Theodore, taking off his hat and nervously passing it from one hand to the other, revealing his closely shaven head. 'We want to do this, really we do. It's just that we've never had quite so much riding on a show going right before. This time, it could cost us our jobs and our family and our friends.'

'I understand, Theodore. I have as much to lose as you all do. Which is why we have to try. Three weeks is all we have and so to get this right we'll use every single second of every single hour of every single day if we have to. Besides, if our three little Pebbles could come up with such a moving performance on the spot like they did, imagine what we can all do with three whole weeks' worth of rehearsal, eh?' Everyone nodded their agreement except for Marigold, who had gradually turned as white as a theatre ghost.

'I have a question,' Mabel said, raising her hand from under her orange sheet of hair.

'Yes, Mabel?' Bam raised an eyebrow when she noticed that she could see two of Mabel's eyes now, which was more than she usually saw when speaking to Mabel.

'How are we going to market the show?'

'Huh?' Morris mumbled.

'You know? How do we promote the show and get people

to buy tickets? We need to spread the word! How are we going to tell everyone what it's about and, more importantly, where and when they can see it?' Mabel shrugged but everyone was looking at her as if she was speaking a different language.

'Mabel, that is a very good question and, considering you seem to be in the know about that kind of thing, why don't you be in charge of that?'

'Huh?' Mabel said, mimicking her brother's facial expression exactly.

'You seem to have a good grasp of all the information the world needs to know about our show, so why don't you be in charge of making it happen?'

'Maybe because I know nothing about promoting a show?'

'What is there to know? It's a show about Pauline, Petrova and Posy Fossil, starring Marigold, Mabel and Morris Pebble, written by Marigold Pebble, and it's showing at the Pebble Theatre three weeks from today.'

'But *how* do we tell people?' Mabel growled.

'Flyers?' Layton suggested.

'People never read flyers. They just throw them in the bin,' Mabel said.

Kitty raised her hand and asked, 'How about posters in tube stations?'

'Far too expensive!' Bam waved her suggestion away.

'The answer you're looking for is social media!' said a voice from the back of the auditorium. 'Sorry to barge in but it seems I came at just the right time.' The Pebble children recognized her bright green shoes before the light from the stage hit her face as she walked up the central aisle.

'Lady!' Mabel rushed down the steps and hugged her tightly.

'Bam, this is Lady. She works at the library and helped me do all my research for the show,' Marigold explained when she caught sight of Bam – who looked as though she was about to yell and hurl Lady from the theatre by the scruff of her coat. Trixabellina had certainly got under Brilliant Aunt Maude's skin!

Bam softened and climbed down from the stage to greet her. 'Well, in that case I owe you several favours! Certainly not the other way around!'

'Are you kidding? I've seen nearly every production this theatre has ever done. My mum used to bring me here when I was a little girl and, now that she's passed away, coming here is the one thing that makes me feel closer to her.' Bam reached out for Lady's hand, which she held in both of hers. 'I would do anything to help save this theatre. Plus, the children are always such a delight when they come to the library and I've got to know Lydia, too . . .' Lydia and Lady shared a warm smile. 'So, please let me help. I promise, it's no trouble at all.'

'Well, when you put it like that . . .' Bam chuckled and the Pebbles cheered, 'Hooray!'

'Right, first things first! I overheard you saying that you

needed a little bit of help getting the word out there, which is exactly my area of expertise!'

'I thought *books* were your expertise?' Mabel teased.

'They *are*.' Lady ruffled Mabel's hair and, to Bam's surprise, Mabel didn't recoil. 'But how do you think I get people to come to the library? I put the word out online of course!' Lady pulled her phone out of her pocket and started tapping on its screen. Bam, whose main form of communication was still sending postcards, felt her palms start to sweat. 'There are millions and millions of people all over the world, and they are all connected by their laptops and mobile phones.'

'Sounds rather daunting . . .' Bam muttered.

'It's simple enough once you get the hang of it! I don't mind using my phone. I can set up an account for the theatre on social media and I'll run it from my phone, but you can log in and use it whenever you visit the library. How does that sound?'

'It sounds like a dream, but is it expensive?' Bam whispered.

'We wouldn't need to spend a single penny. It's all free! My suggestion would be to make a short video and post it online.'

'That sounds simple enough! While I start on rehearsals with the cast – Pebbles, you're in charge of making a video that the whole world will see!' Marigold, Mabel and Morris had a hundred questions but Bam was already busy launching into her plan of action.

Lady laughed and waved at Lydia as Bam dragged her away. 'Right, Pebbles. What's our video going to be?'

'Why don't we film what we did the other day? The first scene of the show!' Morris jumped up and down on the spot.

'Morris, that's a brilliant idea!' Mabel grinned.

'It is?' Morris paused his jumping briefly and then continued, 'I mean, it is!'

'I'm not sure . . .' Lady, Mabel and Morris turned to look at Marigold. The colour still hadn't quite returned to her face.

'Why not? I think it's perfect – and, plus, I'd love to have a sneak preview of the show.' Lady smiled excitedly.

'I've only just got to grips with the idea of all the seats of the theatre being filled with eyes that are all on me on that stage but . . . the whole world?'

'You won't have to see an audience at all, and we won't be broadcasting it live to the nation!' Lady chortled. 'It'll just be the four of us and the camera on my phone.'

'You performed just fine the other day.' Mabel shrugged.

'I know. I don't know what came over me. I think I got a burst of confidence when I overheard *Trixa-ballerina* say that my show wasn't going to be very good.'

'Trixa-who?'

'Trixabellina von Hustle the Third. She's the mean lady who's trying to buy our theatre! She's praying at every step that we fall flat on our faces,' said Morris, scowling.

'Oh, it's her name! I thought you were sneezing! I was about to fetch you a tissue from my purse!' The Pebble children fell about laughing. 'Well, she sounds just charming.' Lady's tongue rolled out of her mouth as if she'd just tasted something disgusting.

'Urgh, she's quite the opposite,' explained Marigold. 'I even think she had something to do with the holes in the roof and all the mice.'

'Mice?!' Lady squealed, threw her head back and hopped on to one foot.

'They're all gone now! We have three theatre cats roaming the theatre, chasing them away. Mack, Maestro and Morticia. But there were hundreds of mice everywhere before we let the cats loose.'

Lady shuddered. 'Well, that's good! Use your defiance of Trixabelini von Shuffle's actions as motivation. Think of her when you feel yourself getting stage fright.'

'Yeah . . .' Marigold nodded, a little bit of pink returning to her cheeks. 'I think that just might work.'

'Good. Now, let's discuss this idea of mine.'

They decided to film their video in front of the theatre, where people could see its name in big bright lights and it was ultra-obvious where to find the show. Lady had run back to the library to fetch a tripod.

'Do you all know what you're going to say?' Lady asked, swiping through her phone to set up a social-media account for the theatre. Marigold, Mabel and Morris quickly ran through their lines, and were happy to find they knew them better than they thought they did. Morris wasn't able to do his fouettés outside on the concrete, but Lady had said they could film a separate video of the dancing.

'That deserves special attention,' Lady had said encouragingly when Morris looked disappointed.

'Mabel . . .' Marigold whispered, repeatedly tugging on Mabel's sleeve and shifting herself behind Mabel's shoulders.

'Whhaaattt?' Mabel moaned, shrugging her sister off, but when Marigold pointed across the street she realized people had stopped to watch what was going on.

'Ah. I should have foreseen this.' Lady scratched her head. 'People do like to be nosey. Shall we head back inside?'

'Yes!' Marigold squeaked but Mabel and Morris both grabbed hold of her arms and stopped her from running back inside.

'No way! We need to do this! This is for the theatre!' Mabel said, grabbing Marigold's hand and pulling her back.

'And us!' shouted Morris, yanking Marigold's other hand with all his might.

'Not with all those people staring!' Marigold shook her head.

'Don't you remember the vow?' Morris widened his eyes at her.

'You took a vow?' Lady interrupted.

'Not us. The Fossils. I've been thinking . . .' Mabel moved

her hair away from her face. Marigold hadn't noticed just how grown-up she was beginning to look, and Morris realized he'd almost forgotten what she actually looked like in among all that hair. 'The Fossils made a vow to each other. *"We three Fossils vow to try to put our names in history books because it's our very own and nobody can say it's because of our grandfathers."* We have to help them keep their vow.'

'Are we really going to do this with all those people watching?' The crowd was starting to cross the road to get a better look.

'There will be a lot more people than that on opening night! Think of this as a dress rehearsal. I'm all set up. Are you ready?' said Lady, her finger poised over the red record button.

Marigold, Mabel and Morris all shared a deep breath but only Marigold scrunched her eyes shut tight before saying, 'Ready!'

'Wait! We need to say the vow!' Morris shouted.

'Really?' Marigold groaned.

'I think that's a lovely idea, Morris,' Lady said as she discreetly hit the record button on her phone. Morris held out his hand, palm facing down. Mabel put her hand on top of his and Marigold followed suit.

'We three Pebbles . . .' Marigold began, still not able to open her eyes for fear of seeing their growing audience.

'. . . vow to try to put the Fossils' story into the history books . . .' Mabel grinned and closed her eyes, too.

'. . . because the Fossil name was their own and no one can say it was because of their grandfathers . . .' Morris said, almost giggling with excitement as he squeezed his eyes shut.

'. . . and even though we never knew them . . .'

'. . . that's what family is for.'

'*Cut!*' Lady yelled. 'I think that's all we need!' All three children snapped open their eyes.

'What?!'

'Were you recording us?'

'We didn't know!'

'I know! Which means you weren't nervous, were you! It was all natural! It came from the heart and it was so beautiful! It's the perfect trailer for your show. The Fossils' vow!' Just then, Lady managed to switch on a light bulb in Marigold's brain and it began to burn brightly.

'The Fossils' vow.'

'Hey, Marigold. That sounds really good.' Mabel turned to face the theatre. 'I reckon I could see that name up there in lights.'

'The Pebble Theatre presents . . .' Morris put on his best announcer voice and waved his hand across the front of the theatre as if he were reading it off the sign. '*The Fossils' Vow*! Written by and starring the talented Marigold Pebble!'

'And the crowd goes wild!' Mabel and Morris ran in circles round Marigold, whooping and cheering as they hoped the crowd would on opening night.

'And also starring her genius sister and dancing prodigy brother, Mabel and Morris Pebble!'

'Three siblings whose name is their own,' Lady said to herself, watching the three Pebbles play with a smile on her face, 'and no one can say it was because of their grandfathers.'

# 24

## Opening Night

Lady's plan had indeed worked wonders. She had shown the Pebbles, Bam and Lydia on the computer at the library (because Bam couldn't see anything on the tiny phone screen), that the video of the children recreating the Fossils' vow had already got over 200,000 views!

'But . . . but . . .' stammered Brilliant Aunt Maude. 'That's more than the population of some small countries! It's a miracle!' That video, and the many photographs that Lady posted on the various social-media accounts, helped tremendously.

'We'll have people calling up to buy tickets in no time!' Mabel threw her fists into the air in triumph.

'Let's not get complacent though, dearies!' Bam warned. 'Even if we happen to sell out our opening night, we need this show to *continue* doing well in order for the theatre to be safe in the long run.'

'Don't worry, Maude.' Lydia grinned. 'When everyone sees how marvellous the show is on opening night, word of mouth will spread the news far and wide. I just know it!'

'Have you noticed how strangely Lydia has been acting recently?' Mabel whispered to Marigold, watching Lydia as she chatted to Lady and swished her hair over her shoulder, her cheeks flushing with colour. 'Yeah, why is her face all weird?' asked Morris.

'Shhh!' Marigold hushed them both. 'It's called a smile! We just rarely see it because she usually looks so worried.'

'About everything,' agreed Mabel.

'All the time.' Morris nodded.

'Maybe some of the money we earn from the show can pay for a holiday for Lydia?' Marigold suggested. Bam had promised to pay the children for their work as actors on the stage. 'All the adults get paid, so there's no reason why you shouldn't either. A job is a job and you deserve to be rewarded for your hard work!' she had said.

'Has she ever had a holiday before?' Morris asked.

'Definitely not since I arrived. She just works and works and works.' Marigold sighed.

'Shall we ask Bam when opening night is over?' Mabel suggested.

'I don't need any money. What am I going to spend it on?' Morris shrugged. Marigold held out her hand and Morris shook it, solidifying their deal.

'I was going to save up for a model of Apollo 13,' huffed Mabel.

'And you still can! I'm sure this show will run for a little while at least and Bam is going to pay us for every week we're in it! Please? For Lydia?' Marigold pouted.

'All right, all right.' Mabel shook Marigold's hand but squeezed a little tighter than Marigold thought necessary.

Rehearsals went as well as they could have expected given the odd stray mouse and the badly patched roof, however, Marigold, Mabel and Morris couldn't believe their luck when six more children arrived to be part of their show. There were lots of laws that meant children couldn't work every day like adults could. This meant three children would share the role of Pauline, three the role of Petrova and three would play Posy. They played games to learn everyone's name and get to know each other and then they took turns asking very hard questions about the characters they were to play, making sure they would be as convincing as possible when onstage in front of an audience. It took them an afternoon of rehearsals to break the ice and then they were an inseparable team. Marigold, Mabel and Morris just *loved* showing them around the theatre and introducing them to the quirky members of their family.

'You're part of the team now. Once a Pebble, always a Pebble!' said Morris with a grin.

Three days before opening night, Marigold, Mabel and Morris were awoken by shuffling outside their room. They ran to the door and opened it to find Bam pacing up and down the corridor in her slippers, tapping her long red nails on every surface.

'Is everything all right, Bam?' Marigold yawned.

'Sorry, little ones. I didn't mean to wake you. Just a little nervous, that's all.'

'Why? Isn't everything going according to plan?' asked Mabel, catching Marigold's yawn. They might have all had bleary eyes but they could still see that Bam looked sheepish.

'No secrets,' Morris said.

'Well, it's just . . . we've not had very many people call up to buy tickets. Lady's pictures and videos have had so many . . . What do you call them? Hits? But only about twenty people so far are actually coming.'

'Give it time?' suggested Marigold weakly.

'I'm afraid time is something we just don't have.' Bam sighed and sent them back to bed with knots in their stomachs.

★

Opening night was also the last night of the summer holidays and while the other children hired for the show would soon get their time to shine, the first show belonged to the Pebbles. It came around so fast that they all felt a little bit giddy, but no one was as nervous as Bam.

'*EVERYONE!*' Her voice squealed over the tannoy. '*Everyone outside the front of the theatre. Now!*' The Pebbles and Lydia were all having dinner in the hour or two between the final dress rehearsal and the first performance. The dress rehearsal had its glitches but nothing that couldn't be sorted before the evening. Bam didn't sound like she wanted to be kept waiting so they scurried outside and joined the rest of the theatre family. They found Bam and Lady standing in front of one of the posters for *The Fossils' Vow*. Bam was hopping from foot to foot with excitement she could barely contain.

'My soup's getting cold . . .' Layton pouted.

'It'll only be a minute. Lady has an announcement!' Bam shrugged and handed over to Lady, who couldn't stop herself from smiling.

'I promise you all that you won't want to miss this. Are you all here? Good. I have some news. Close your eyes.' Marigold, Mabel and Morris all looked at each other, their stomachs somersaulting in unison.

'Come on, come on!' Bam urged them all. 'Do as she says! Close your eyes!' They all did as they were told. Lady began to move about. They could hear rustling and even Lady giggling to herself.

After a few moments, Lady yelled, 'Now . . . *OPEN*!'

When they opened their eyes, they all gasped and then cheered – but no one shrieked as loud as Bam. Across the centre of the poster for their wonderful show, Lady had stuck a giant red sticker that said SOLD OUT.

'Oh, Lady! Really?' Lydia clasped her hands over her heart.

'But how?!' Bam's hands were trembling as she clasped them over her mouth.

'When I set up all the social media, I also set up a long-overdue website for the theatre and along with it . . . a booking page. Whenever I posted about *The Fossils' Vow*, I always made sure to include the link that would send people straight to buy tickets. Opening night was sold out within a few hours but I wanted it to be a surprise. I also didn't want to make anyone more nervous than they needed to be,' Lady added as she glanced at Dawson's face, now as white as a theatre ghost.

'Are you all right, darling?' Dante gave Dawson's arm a little shake, but he simply flapped his mouth open and closed like a goldfish.

'This theatre has never been full.' Dawson's voice trembled as he spoke. 'It's meant to be a safe space. Bam, you promised me it was a safe space!' he boomed.

'It's been a safe space for you to build your confidence for far longer than either of us ever expected. Be thankful for the years you've had. Now it's time to shine,' she said in a tone that said: 'And that's that.' Dawson closed his mouth, but the colour did not return to his cheeks.

'I thought *the end* were my two favourite words this month after Marigold finished the play . . .' Bam smiled. 'But *sold out* really takes the cake!'

Marigold, Mabel and Morris had seen many opening nights come and go at the Pebble Theatre but none of them had ever felt this electric. It was as though you could hear the theatre humming from a mile away, drawing you closer and closer, and it grew louder and louder until you burst through the doors of the auditorium with your ticket clutched in your hand. Marigold had to keep running outside to the front of the theatre to make sure she hadn't lost her mind and there really was a big red SOLD OUT sticker across the poster for her play. Every time she looked at it she felt dizzy.

It was for this reason that, when 'act one beginners' was called out across the tannoy (the call five minutes before the show starts to anyone in the beginning of the show to come to the stage and get into position), Marigold was leaning over the toilet bowl, her head spinning and her stomach somersaulting, certain she was going to be sick despite the fact she hadn't eaten a single thing all day.

'Marigold?' Lydia knocked on the door and, after a few moments of Marigold holding her breath pretending she wasn't in there, Lydia tried the door handle anyway. Marigold inwardly cursed herself for having a fear of getting trapped in the bathroom and not locking the door.

'Nervous?' Lydia said, dropping to her knees and stroking Marigold's back like she used to when Marigold was really little. Marigold could barely nod her head because she was already shaking so much.

'Butterflies are fine as long as they fly in formation. That's what Bam always says. And you know she's always right.'

That managed to coax a smile out of Marigold but the nerves made her tummy flip once more and it quickly faded.

'Oh, Marigold. You've come so far, it'd be such a shame to turn back now.'

'I know, I know,' Marigold groaned.

She thought about all the times she didn't believe in herself and all the times she didn't think she could do what everyone was asking of her. She thought back to the times she had sat with her forehead pressed against the blank pages in her notebook when she was certain she would never be able to write an entire play. Then she thought about all the times everyone else had believed in her even when she was telling herself '*I can't do this*'. And about all the times she had done it anyway. And then about the fact that it was the sold-out opening night of *her* show. Suddenly, before she even knew it herself, Marigold was on her feet.

'I can do this, I think. No, I know I can do this.' Marigold swallowed hard, took several deep breaths and, on shaky legs, made her way to the stage.

'Oh, my sweet girl! You've got this, Marigold!' Bam whispered from the wing as Marigold took her place behind the curtain, centre stage. Mabel and Morris appeared by Bam's side and both gave her big grins and thumbs up. All of a sudden, the small band in the orchestra stopped warming up and the audience went silent.

'What's going on? Are we ready to start?' Marigold panicked.

'This happens. It's almost as though everyone senses at the same moment that the show is about to begin and falls silent. One of the magical things about the theatre!' Lydia explained.

The butterflies in Marigold's tummy certainly weren't flying in formation because they were trying to get out of her mouth. 'I want to be sick!'

'Deep breaths! This is *your* show, Marigold. You hold the power!' Bam said.

'Yeah, if you screw up, they've never seen this show before so how will they know?' Mabel shrugged.

'Weirdly, that helps. Thanks, Mabel!'

'Besides.' Bam grinned. 'They've already purchased their tickets and we've already got their money – so, as long as we don't cancel, we're quids in! Hoorah!'

'*MAUDE!*' Lydia shout-whispered. It was very rare that Bam let the children see the side of her that was a ruthless producer, but whenever she did it always made them laugh – mostly because of how much it wound Lydia up.

'Stand by, we have clearance from front of house.' Lydia spoke into her headset and then cupped a hand over the microphone. 'It's time? Are you ready?'

Marigold thought about everything that had led up to this moment and how triumphant this night could be if she just believed in herself like Bam, Lydia, Mabel and Morris believed in her.

'We're right behind you, Marigold!' said a voice from inside the set of Great-uncle Matthew's house, which she was standing in front of. She squinted through the darkness and saw Dawson waving at her from one of its windows. One by one all the cast's faces appeared from behind the scenery and gave her nods of encouragement. 'Literally and figuratively!'

'OK.' Marigold actually managed to smile as she felt the butterflies in her stomach calm their fluttering for a moment, knowing that she had a whole team of wonderful people supporting her. A family who were with her every step of the way. 'I'm ready.'

And the curtain rose.

# 25

## Plunged into Darkness

The show went as smoothly as an opening night could go. There were minor stumbles over lines, and literal stumbles as Kitty and Claudia bumped into each other while playing Posy's dancing classmates, but Bam stood at the back of the stalls, beaming with pride. Everyone laughed and cried in all the right places and the three most precious Pebbles in her collection were the reason why. Marigold had wowed everyone with her clever writing and beautiful narration of the story. Mabel had impressed with her confident acting and brilliant portrayal of the fearless Petrova, and Morris had certainly stolen the show with his perfect pirouettes. The rest of the theatre family had rallied around and pulled together to form an impeccable cast. Layton was marvellously funny as Great-uncle Matthew and even managed to remember most of his lines. However, there was one moment right near the beginning where he faltered.

'It's a baby, of course!' he said, rocking the bundle of blankets in his arms that was meant to represent baby Pauline. 'And her name is . . .' He paused for only a few seconds, but it felt like a lifetime. Bam's heart leapt into her mouth and everyone on stage and behind the scenes held their breath. Was this the moment the show would fall apart? And so close to the start? 'And her name is . . .'

'Pauline!' Morris muttered under his breath in the wings. 'Her name is Pauline! How's he forgotten one of the most important parts of the show?'

'Her name . . . her name is . . .' Beads of sweat had begun to drip down his face. 'Her . . . name . . . is . . .' Just as Cora was about to give Layton a prompt from her desk in the wings, he shouted, *'Pauline! Her name is Pauline!* Yes! Yes, that's it!' Bam let out a great sigh of relief along with the rest of the theatre and luckily it was plain sailing from there onwards. If Dawson was nervous, it certainly didn't show on stage. He was awfully dashing as Mr Simpson, the man who taught Petrova everything she knew about cars, and Kitty and Claudia made a wonderful Sylvia and Nana, the stalwart women who looked after the Fossil sisters. Marigold peeped out from behind the curtain during the interval and spotted Winifred's pink bob straight away. She was sitting in the front row of the dress circle and she'd had to remove her glasses to be able to wipe the tears from her eyes, but even though she was clearly emotional she was grinning from ear to ear. *Certainly a good sign*, Marigold thought. During the interval Bam skulked in the shadows nursing a very stiff drink, hoping to eavesdrop on the audience's conversations. However, she had barely even taken a sip when someone pounced on her.

'Maude, darling!' Bam didn't recognize this person, but pretended she did as he ran over and air-kissed round her face. He was a short, squat bald man in a dark blue suit, and he was wearing thick-rimmed black glasses. She couldn't help but notice he had a small notepad and pen wedged into his top pocket. Maude's back stiffened and she switched her brain into producer mode, making certain to think very carefully about her answers to whatever this journalist might ask her. 'Such a risk you took on such a young child!' he tutted.

'No risk at all! Marigold is one of London's finest writers and the evidence is right up there on that stage!' Her laugh trilled through the air between them but, as she tried to move away, he clung to her like a bad smell.

'She's only a child, though.'

'"*Only* a child"?' Bam tutted back at him in the same

disapproving manner. 'There's no *only* about it. Children often see things that go unseen by us silly adults and have the fearlessness to speak about it. A fearlessness people like us have replaced with worry and concern for things that never really mattered in the first place.' Bam tried to move away once more, but this time the journalist placed a hand on her arm and she tensed underneath his grip.

'I'm just saying it seems like she's had a bit of a helping hand with all this. It can't have been all *her*. She's barely even in double digits. What sort of game are you playing?' Bam snatched her arm away and took a deep breath before continuing, remembering to choose every word very carefully in case what she said would appear in the papers tomorrow.

'Everyone needs a helping hand at some point along the way, *sir*. It doesn't make our achievements any less our own.'

'But – but . . .' he stammered.

'If I were you, I'd be far more preoccupied with working out why I'm so obsessed with dismantling the successes of a twelve-year-old girl.' Bam finally threw caution to the wind and couldn't help but let him have it. 'Goodness me. As soon as someone lights a candle in this cold, dark world it seems there's always someone like *you* around to try and blow it out. It's lucky Marigold has a wonderful group of people around her to protect her spark at all costs.' The journalist had turned a very odd colour, somewhere between pink and orange, and Bam was sure a blood vessel in his eye was about to burst.

'I'll be writing about this tomorrow. I have a very successful blog, you know!' he spat.

'I'm sure all three of your readers will be thrilled. If they're anything like you, make sure to tell them not to come!' Finally, the man had run out of things to say and she broke away. Luckily, for the rest of the interval she was met with only kindness and love and, when the lights went down, the audience quickly fell silent, ready to devour the second act.

Marigold, Mabel and Morris had certainly hit their stride and not only were they doing superbly but they also seemed to be having an awful lot of fun. Growing up in a theatre had certainly made them naturals at acting. Marigold and Morris were just about to launch into the final scene which also happened to be Bam's favourite. It was the scene in which Pauline and Posy think Petrova went down in her plane and won't be coming home. It never failed to make Bam tearful.

'Pauline . . . I think we have to stop waiting and move on,' Morris said, hugging a pair of ballet shoes to his chest.

'I know, Posy.' Marigold pulled Morris to her, held him close, and they both closed their eyes. 'I just hope Petrova knows that, even though she was on her own, she wasn't alone.' It was at this moment that Mabel, playing Petrova, was supposed to appear on the stage and the audience was supposed to erupt into cheers and whoops as Petrova returned home to her sisters. Instead, the entire theatre was abruptly plunged into darkness. Silence followed and then a murmur of confusion.

'Is this meant to happen?'

'Is this part of the show?'

People whispered back and forth as Bam fumbled her way down the side aisle and through the pass door that led into the stage left wing.

'What's going on?!' she hissed, feeling around for something to grab on to.

'Ouch, that was my hair!'

'Sorry, Marigold. Where's Lydia?'

'Here!' Lydia's voice said very close to Bam's ear.

'*AHH!*' Bam screamed and jumped away, landing on Morris's toe. He then also screamed.

'We've lost power, Bam. We're trying to find out why, but it may take a while to sort it out and get it back up and running.' Lydia's voice was high-pitched and frantic.

'We don't have a while! It takes mere minutes for an audience to start losing interest!'

'I've got an idea!' Mabel said from near where Marigold was standing. 'I need Dante!'

'I'm here.' Dante found Mabel's hand and she began to lead him away from the group. 'What are we doing?'

'I think it's time we introduce our friend Pepper to the gang, don't you?'

'Mabel, you're a genius! Bam, this shouldn't take too long.'

'Who's Pepper?! Does she know how to get the power back up and running? Why have I never met her before?' But neither Mabel nor Dante answered because they had scuttled off to the cellar, moving by the light of Dante's phone torch, to fetch everything they needed to recreate Dante's ghost illusion. When Mabel got back to them with a torch in hand, the audience was chattering noisily among themselves, clearly disgruntled with the delay in the performance. Bam was also very displeased.

'Where have you been?! People are threatening to get up and leave!' Bam growled.

'It's OK – we have a plan. Marigold, you need to go out there and improvise the last scene of the show!'

'Improvise? Why?'

'Nothing's working! No microphones, no lights, nothing! We can't have the whole cast wandering out willy-nilly! No one knows the story better than you.'

Everyone held their breath, waiting for Marigold to tell them she couldn't possibly do it and that she was too scared. Instead, she surprised them all. 'Yeah, I can do that. Don't worry, I've got this.' Morris's mouth flopped open like a codfish.

'Who are you and what have you done with my sister?'

'As much as I *love* the new and improved Marigold, can we talk about it later? We've got a show to finish.' Mabel rolled up her sleeves.

'Where's Dante?' Lydia asked.

'He's setting up.'

'Setting up what?!' Bam shrieked. 'Mabel, if you don't tell me what's going on *right now* –'

'Marigold, go to Dante and he's going to tell you exactly where to stand.' Mabel ignored Bam's hysterics, which only made her more hysterical. Marigold could see her shaking with frustration in the light from Mabel's torch. 'It's actually a real shame you're not terrified of the audience any more, because this would have been a great solution.'

'What on earth are you talking about?' Marigold asked, looking at her sister with proud admiration.

'Just trust me, sis!'

'What can I do? I want to help!' Morris hopped from foot to foot, eager to be in on the action.

'And you will. We all will. Marigold, go and get into position while I explain to Bam how this show is going to go out with a bang!'

'This way, m'lady.' Dante appeared at Marigold's side and offered her his hand, which she gratefully took as he was able to light her way with a torch.

'Should I be worried?' She looked at him sideways to see he was grinning from ear to ear like a child on Christmas Day.

'Not in the slightest. If anything, this might be the easiest thing you've done all night.'

Dante led Marigold up the stairs behind the set of

223

Great-uncle Matthew's house. There were three windows at the top of the house where Dante had set up three big panes of glass at a funny angle.

'Now, Marigold, you stand here and face the glass.' He pointed to a spot on the floor behind the set where the audience wouldn't see her.

'But . . . why? I won't be seen here.'

'You will! Give me some credit! This illusion is over one hundred and fifty years old! When I light you with this big battery-powered light here, your reflection in the glass will appear and face the audience.'

'So . . . I don't have to look at the audience at all?'

'Exactly!' Dante flipped a switch. The light was pointed up towards her face and suddenly her reflection appeared in the glass and her eyes widened in wonder.

'Wow . . . I could get used to this!' she said, waving to herself.

'I thought you might say that!' Dante laughed.

'But . . . why are we using this illusion anyway?'

'Well, by turning the light on and off, I can make your reflection appear and disappear. So Mabel figured that since Pauline, Petrova and Posy are no longer around, why not give the audience the ghosts they came to see?' They were both startled by the familiar rattle of the curtain rising. Brilliant Aunt Maude was clearly panicking in the wings and wanted things to continue as quickly as possible to avoid disaster. The crowd fell silent and Marigold knew it was up to her, and Dante's brilliant magic trick, to save the show and, with it, the theatre. Marigold was suddenly struck by how calm she was when she wasn't able to see the audience, and she couldn't stop herself from smiling. Unhindered by nerves, Marigold was able to be the best writer she could be, even if she was put on the spot.

'Dearest audience. Tonight, darkness fell over our show, just as it fell over Pauline and Posy when Petrova and her plane disappeared over enemy lines. You'll be pleased to know Pauline's and Posy's desperate sadness was short-lived because . . . Petrova returned.' The audience gasped in unison, then let out a sigh of relief and burst into applause and cheers. Marigold didn't understand why until her eyes adjusted to beyond her own reflection and she saw Mabel with her back to her, standing in a similar position at the next window along, another battery-powered light pointing up at her face. She had appeared miraculously out of thin air as Petrova, returning home.

'When Pauline, Petrova and Posy were children, they chose their own name and that name was Fossil. It belonged to them and no one else – and in that name they made a vow.' Marigold discreetly made a signal with her hand and pointed to the window behind her. She heard Morris scramble up the steps and take his position in front of the glass and the audience gasped again as Dante faded his light up, making him appear to the audience. 'We three Fossils . . .' Marigold began, and Mabel and Morris joined in with her, '. . . vow to try to put our names in history books because it's our very own and nobody can say it's because of our grandfathers.'

'Posy had many ballets written for her and danced all over the world. Petrova became one of a few female pilots and Pauline became a Hollywood star. However, despite their great achievements, they aren't famous today. Which is why I, Marigold Pebble . . .'

'And I, Mabel Pebble . . .'

'And I, Morris Pebble . . .'

'Vow to uphold their vow and continue telling their story. You may ask why three children would do such a thing for three people they never knew. It is because their story is *our* story. Three orphans brought together by fate. We Pebbles are family not by blood or marriage. We are family by love and kindness. We are family because we *say* we are family. And so, through us, Pauline, Petrova and Posy live on . . . Forever.' Marigold signalled once more. Dante slowly faded down the lights and with them the ghostly reflections of Marigold, Mabel and Morris. There was a moment of stillness in the auditorium. The three Pebbles chanced a glance at each other. Marigold felt her heart suddenly begin to race and her eyes well up, thinking that Mabel's plan hadn't worked or that her words hadn't made enough of an impact to save the theatre. Then, in one great roar, the audience erupted.

'*BRAVO! BRAVO! BRAVO!*' The noise was so deafening, Morris had to put his hands over his ears but he was laughing, even so. Mabel jumped up and down, shaking the set as she cheered, '*YES! WE DID IT!*' And Marigold *did* burst into tears, but they were happy ones. Very happy ones, indeed.

# 26

# Trixabellina von Hustle the Third

The curtain fell on a triumphant performance, despite its hitches, and Marigold, Mabel and Morris were swept into a frenzy of handshakes and hugs from the cast and crew of the Pebble Theatre.

'I don't want to speak too soon but I think we actually managed to save the theatre.' Bam grinned. 'Mabel, your quick thinking tonight saved the show. You should be incredibly proud of yourself. I know we are.'

'Me?' Mabel quickly pulled her hair in front of her face. 'Huh . . . I just wanted to help!' She shrugged.

'And you did help, tremendously. If it wasn't for you summoning the ghosts of Pauline, Petrova and Posy, I don't know what we would have done!'

'I can't see this show closing for a long, long time.' Lydia smiled with tears in her eyes.

'We owe all three of you, in fact, an indefinite debt of gratitude.' Bam hugged them individually and then all together.

'Bravo! Bravo!' Lady and Winifred joined them on stage from the auditorium.

'Oh, my goodness!' Winifred was draped in a cape made of what looked like an old red velvet theatre curtain. 'I've not had an evening quite so exciting in all my life! And that includes the night I was thrown on as Alice in place of Pauline.' Winifred wrapped her arms (and her cape!) round Marigold. 'You should be so proud of yourself. You're a real talent! Now, do you have representation? Because I think I could really use someone like –'

'Ah, ah, ah, Winifred!' Bam waggled her finger at Winifred. 'You'll have to negotiate all that with me, I'm afraid.'

'I *was* afraid of that. I bet you drive a hard bargain, Maude. But fine. I'm glad you've got good people looking out for you, Marigold.'

'You really were so marvellous. I'm so proud of you all!' Lady gave all three Pebbles a kiss on the cheek, leaving behind big red lipstick marks.

'None of it could have been done without all your help, Lady. We can't thank you enough,' said Morris.

'That's what librarians are for! But . . . why was there a power cut? That didn't happen in the dress rehearsal!' Lady asked.

'I think I might know why . . .' Theodore stomped on to the stage in his big black boots, dragging in tow – and looking quite terrified – none other than Trixabellina von Hustle the Third, who looked quite terrified. 'I found this one by the main power supply. It'll take forever to fix it all!'

'Well, well, well, look what the theatre cat dragged in,' said Lydia, stepping in front of the children. 'Looks like we had one big rat as well as lots of little mice.'

'All right, all right.' Trixabellina held up her hands. Her American accent dissolved and was replaced with a very familiar English one.

'What's happened to your voice?' Theo asked.

'What's going on?' Lydia crossed her arms and gave Trixabellina her best stern stare – the one that made the three Pebbles go cold.

'Let me explain.' Trixabellina took off her sunglasses and suddenly her face became much softer than before.

'You don't need to explain!' Bam yelled. 'You were trying to drive us out of this theatre so you could swipe it out from under us and turn it into an eight-bedroom mansion all for yourself! All the mice and the holes in the roof and the power going out . . . it was all you, wasn't it?'

'Yes, it was, but I promise everything that's broken will be fixed.' Marigold noticed that she actually looked quite . . . sorry. She recognized that look from whenever Morris had accidentally broken something.

'Too right it'll be fixed!'

'Bam . . . I think we should hear her out.'

'Thank you, Marigold,' Trixabellina said, and Theodore finally let go of the scruff of her nice pink jacket. 'My real name is Trixie. Trixie Fossil. Well, that's my stage name, at least. You see, I'm an actress and Trixabellina might have been my most convincing role yet.'

'You're . . . you're a Fossil?' Mabel stammered.

'I'm Pauline Fossil's granddaughter.' She smiled and the Pebbles gasped.

'. . . Woah.'

'I thought you might say that.' Trixie laughed.

'Is your grandmother still alive?' Mabel asked loudly. Marigold nudged her bold sister.

'She isn't, I'm afraid, but just look at what she's left behind! People are still talking about her even after she's gone.'

'And Posy and Petrova?' Morris's puppy-dog eyes were almost too much for Trixie to bear.

'I'm sorry, little ones. I suppose you were hoping to meet

them? You'll have to settle for their daughters and granddaughters. Just you wait until I tell them all how amazing you were tonight.' She batted Morris playfully on the shoulder and he lit up.

'But why did you pretend to be someone so awful?' Marigold was perplexed by the real Trixie's kindness.

'Well, the Pebble Theatre was my grandma's favourite theatre. Back when it was the Windmill. She used to take my mum to all the shows that played here and then my mum brought me when I was little. When I heard it was in trouble, I knew I had to try and help save it.'

'But you didn't help. You tried to destroy our chances of saving our theatre,' Bam accused.

'Did I?' Trixie shrugged and gestured to the audience that was still cheering beyond the curtain. 'All good actresses do their research before they launch into a new role, and I discovered that your Brilliant Aunt Maude here was all set to shut up shop and sell. I figured with such a tight-knit family, she probably already had a whole host of people around her who would support her decision to sell the theatre, even if they knew in their heart of hearts it wasn't the right thing to do.' Bam flushed pink. 'It was since I came along that changed, wasn't it?'

'Well . . . well . . . you went and got me all steamed up, didn't you? I wasn't about to hand my theatre over to the likes of someone like you.'

'Someone like Trixabellina,' Marigold corrected her aunt.

'Exactly.' Trixie winked at Marigold. 'My grandma never would have forgiven me for not doing all I could to save her favourite theatre. I would have felt guilty every time I passed the spot of the old Pebble Theatre that was now a cinema or a takeaway. It would have broken my heart because I know it would have broken hers. So, I invented Trixabellina von Hustle the Third to scare you into doing all you could to stop someone so horrible from having it. You have to admit . . . it worked.' Trixie clutched her giant sunglasses with sweaty hands and Marigold could see her legs were beginning to tremble in her high heels. Marigold completely understood that standing and waiting for the judgement of Aunt Maude was probably more terrifying than standing on stage in front of a packed-out audience.

'But what about tonight? The power cut? If you wanted to save the theatre, why did you try and ruin our one chance of success?' Bam asked.

'Ah, now, that wasn't me. That was unfortunately your rickety old theatre not used to having this many people under its roof. I was actually trying to fix the problem and probably would have succeeded had I not been pulled away quite so violently . . .'

'Oh!' Theo gasped. 'I'm so sorry!' His bottom lip began to tremble.

'You were doing what you thought was best.' Trixie

smiled. Everyone was looking at Bam and waiting for her to say something. A few of them were even waiting for her to start yelling. Instead, she walked right up to Trixie, wrapped her arms round her and held her tightly.

'Thank you for making me fight for the things I love the most,' Bam whispered, and everyone was surprised to see that she didn't swallow down the lump in her throat or hold back her tears like she so often did. They flowed freely down her cheeks, along with her mascara. 'Not just the theatre – at the end of the day, that's just bricks and mortar, but the family within it. Thank you, Trixie Fossil. Your grandma would be proud.' Trixie let herself give in and sank into Bam's arms, also shedding tears of her own. Then, one by one, each member of the Pebble Theatre family joined the huddle, all emotional in their own way but no one blubbed louder than Theodore.

'I just love a happy ending!'

'We've had enough of endings,' said Bam, her voice muffled from the centre of the hug. 'This, my friends, is a beginning.'

# 27

# A Happy Ending

*The Fossils' Vow* was booked solidly for six months. The Pebble Theatre was indeed saved. They celebrated in the kitchen the next morning before school. Lady brought over all the newspapers that gave their show four- and five-star reviews and they laid them all out on the kitchen table in a dazzling display. They ate eggs and bacon and marmalade on toast but on this particular morning, the children had a surprise for Lydia.

'What's all this about?' Lydia put down her mug when Marigold, Mabel and Morris approached her, all standing in a straight line with their hands behind their backs, giggling uncontrollably. 'This all looks very suspicious . . .'

'The children have something for you.' Bam laughed. 'And before you begin to protest, I also tried to talk them out of it but they absolutely insisted.'

'You didn't try to talk us out of it.' Morris shook his head. 'You told us it was a great idea – *OUCH*! Why did you kick me, Mabel?!'

'Come on, then.' Lydia smiled. 'Don't keep me in suspense. What are you three up to?' With an awkward shuffle, the Pebble children moved out of the way to reveal a giant train ticket that they had made themselves out of an old cardboard box. They'd sprinkled it in gold and silver glitter and underneath the word DESTINATION they had written ANYWHERE YOU LIKE. 'What on earth is this?'

'Oh, Lydia, please accept it?' Marigold begged. 'We can't remember the last time you had a holiday. We don't even know if you've ever had one at all! So we clubbed together the money that Bam paid us for our first week in showbiz and we want to give it to you so you can go anywhere you want.'

'Oh, how sweet!' Lady beamed.

'What with Bam being pretty stingy though, we can only afford to send you somewhere in the UK –' Mabel's insolence was stifled by Bam covering her mouth.

'What Mabel means to say,' Bam interjected, 'is that anywhere away from this theatre, even for a few days, is still a holiday. I've always said you work too hard.'

'Are you lot trying to get rid of me?' Lydia eyed them.

'Of course not!' Marigold took Lydia's hand. 'We just want to say thank you. For helping to save the theatre but mostly . . . for everything you've done for us since Bam found us.'

'All the things we've never said thank you for before,' said Mabel.

'You deserve it!' Morris kissed Lydia on the cheek.

'Well . . .' Lydia said, and everyone held their breath, unsure of what she was going to say, 'I've always wanted to go to Edinburgh!'

'Hooray!' the children cheered and gave her the giant train ticket, which she gratefully took.

'I'll go on holiday on one condition . . . That you all come with me? After the show finishes, of course,' she added as Bam began to protest. 'Next year's summer holiday, perhaps? Oh please, it wouldn't be a proper holiday if you all weren't there, too.'

'Oh, can we, Bam? Can we?' the children pleaded.

'I don't see why not! That sounds like a brilliant idea! As long as there's room for me too.'

'Of course but . . . just so you know, that also includes Lady . . .' Lydia said a little quietly.

'Lady?' Bam blinked.

'Yes.' Lydia reached across the kitchen table and took Lady's hand and stroked the back of it with her thumb. 'I don't think I've ever met someone quite as wonderful as Lady before. I knew right from the moment I met her.'

'So did I,' said Lady, unable to contain her laughter. Then Lydia smiled in the way the children had noticed before and suddenly they realized why. She was in love. The revelation was interrupted by a loud wailing noise coming from Bam, who was holding a hanky to her nose and blowing very loudly.

'Oh, yes, Lydia,' she bawled. 'This . . . you two . . .' She pointed at their entwined fingers and smiled through her tears. 'It's perfect! I couldn't be happier for you! Lady, please come with us?'

'Yes, please, come with us to Edinburgh, Lady!' they chimed.

'Well, if you're sure . . .' Lady nodded. They all cheered once more and hugged Lydia and Lady.

'Oh, Morris! Before I forget, something came for you in the post today,' said Lydia.

'Post? For me? But I *never* get post!' Lydia pointed to the kitchen table where a letter was propped up in the toast rack between two slices of toast. 'Who's it from?'

'Usually you open letters to find out who they're from,' Mabel teased. Morris tore into the envelope and pulled out a neatly folded thick sheet of what looked more like parchment than paper.

'It doesn't have a stamp.' Morris turned it over in his hands. 'It must have been hand-delivered!'

'Well, don't keep us waiting! What does it say?' Marigold asked, and Morris opened it and began to read.

*Dear Master Pebble,*

*The Posy Fossil Academy of Dance was designed to find young people with great potential and an enthusiasm for dance. We help to hone their natural flair into a talent that will give them a promising future. As you well know, Trixie Fossil has been watching you for the last few weeks and, upon her recommendation, I purchased a ticket to last night's performance of The Fossils' Vow. I must say, I have never seen a young person with such elegance, poise and natural instinct. So it is with great delight that I write to you to offer you a full scholarship to our school. I think you would make a marvellous addition and I eagerly await your response.*

*Yours truly . . . impressed,*

*Phoebe Fossil*

*(Posy's granddaughter)*

There was stunned silence as Morris read and reread the letter at least three more times before looking up at his family, whose mouths were hanging open.

'Morris . . .' Marigold breathed.

'Wow . . .' whispered Mabel.

'Can I go?' Morris looked at Lydia and Bam with hope-filled eyes and bated breath.

'What a ridiculous question!' snapped Bam with a stern look. 'You *have* to go.' Then she said, her face softening into a grin, 'You've been summoned by destiny and she rarely takes no for an answer.'

'Oh, Brilliant Aunt Maude! This is the most brilliant you've ever been! Thank you, thank you, thank you!'

'Congratulations!' Marigold, Mabel and Lydia cried.

'I think this calls for hot chocolate!' shouted Bam.

'At seven-thirty in the morning?'

'Chocolate always tastes better when it's early!'

As Marigold sipped her hot chocolate, her eyes glanced over one of their many glowing reviews and Dawson's name jumped out at her. She decided to read it a little more closely.

**While the children are of course the stars of the show, there is someone else who shone just as brightly. Dawson Sanders, playing Mr Simpson, was simply exquisite. Where he's been hiding all these years, I don't know. But now that he's been unearthed, I urge you all to see his wonderful performance in *The Fossils' Vow*, currently playing at the Pebble Theatre. I truly believe a star has been born.**

After school, shortly before showtime that evening, Marigold rapped on Dawson's dressing-room door.

'What a lovely surprise!' Dante said as he welcomed her in. Dawson was staring intently at himself in the mirror, dabbing stage make-up on to his face with a sponge.

'I won't take up too much of your time,' Marigold promised. 'I just wanted to give you a present.'

'A present?' Dawson raised an eyebrow.

'Would you mind . . . closing your eyes?' she asked, and Dawson obliged with a small smile. Dante helped her quietly open the empty cabinet in the corner and she gently placed something inside and closed the door. 'Annnnd open!' Marigold and Dante stood either side of the cabinet, their arms outstretched, fluttering their jazz hands to frame the new addition. 'Ta-da!' Marigold cried with a grin.

'What is it?' Dawson stood and knelt down in front of the glass to get a closer look. On the top shelf, in a golden frame, sat the glowing review highlighting all the wonderful things said about Dawson's performance. Marigold watched his face as he read and a lump began to form in her throat as his eyes quickly filled with tears.

'You see, Dawson? It's never too late,' Dante said, his eyes also glistening.

'I know it's not an award.' Marigold shrugged. 'But it's proof that one day it could be, right?' Dante winked at her, no longer able to speak through his emotion. Dawson nodded and, true to form, also said nothing. However, he pulled Marigold towards him and hugged her as tightly as he could, hoping it said everything he could not.

The following summer, on their special holiday in Edinburgh, Bam insisted they visit Portobello Beach as it was such a warm and sunny day.

'None of you are allowed home until you've all found a pebble to take back to the theatre!' she declared, as she sat herself in a beach chair with a portion of seaside chips wrapped in paper, a little wooden fork sticking out of the top, and the smell of salt and vinegar making her mouth water. However, it seemed that no one was listening. Lydia and Lady were sitting together on a towel engrossed in deep conversation, smiling and laughing more than the children had ever seen Lydia smile and laugh before. Marigold's nose was stuck in her notebook, working on a new play all about how three siblings had once saved a theatre from the clutches of a woman dressed all in pink. Mabel had built herself a kite that was apparently the perfect shape and size to catch the wind just right and fly for hours. Her tongue was sticking out of her mouth in concentration as she ran along the beach with the kite in tow. They all cheered as it caught a gust and lifted perfectly into the air on her first try. Morris was waist deep in the waves, letting the water lift him into the air for long enough to point his feet and perfect the latest balletic move he'd learnt at the Posy Fossil Academy of Dance. Everyone was happier than they'd ever been before and no one seemed to have a care in the world.

And so, because of Morris's elegant feet, Mabel's quick thinking and Marigold's imagination, the theatre was saved and the family with it. Morris was to learn to be a dancer, Mabel would continue out-thinking everyone in the room, and Marigold had a new-found confidence when it came to her writing. No one knows what the future holds but maybe the Pebbles would one day get their name into the history books. If they did, it would be because their name was their own and nobody could say it was because of their grandfathers.

**THE END**

# Acknowledgements

There's always a huge amount of people who make an idea the reality you now hold in your hands so I'm going to try to keep this brief while also doing my best to not forget anyone!

Huge love and thanks to everyone at Puffin. Millie Lean, Kathy Webb, Simon Armstrong, Hannah Bradridge, Andrea Bowie and the wonderful Carmen McCullough, thank you for welcoming me to the Puffin family and for helping to get the Pebble Theatre up and running. To Kiersten Eagan and Andrea Kearney, thank you for making the book look stunning and for bringing the Pebbles to life!

As always, a great, big warm hug to my book agent, Hannah Ferguson. Thank you for holding my hand through these sometimes-daunting processes! You make everything feel very calm and for that, I couldn't be more thankful. Big hugs also to my team at Curtis Brown. Alastair, Helen, Ronan, Emma, Emily, Fran and Jess. Thanks for having my back.

Big love as ever to my family! Mum, Dad, Nan, Grandad, Tom, Gi and especially my three gremlin nephews, Buzz, Buddy and Max. If you three like the book, then it is officially a success!

Thanks to my wonderful friends who make my life so magical and keep me going. Scott Paige, Mollie Melia Redgrave, Paul Bradshaw, Matt Mcdonald, Matt Gillett, Celinde Schoenmaker, Ben Forster, Ramin Karimloo, Alex Banks, Emma Kingston, Rob Houchen, Johnny and Lucy Vickers, Louise Jones, Louise Pentland, Sophie Isaacs, Becky Lock and of course my wonderful Oliver Ormson, who puts up with the majority of my faffing and stressing. I couldn't love you more! If I've managed to forget anyone, please know you are still very loved!

It is the experiences I had as a child in theatre that helped bring this story to life. So I would like to say thank you to the 2001 cast of *Les Mis* at the Palace Theatre, the 2002 cast of *Chitty Chitty Bang Bang* at the Palladium and the 2004 cast of *Mary Poppins* at the Prince Edward. Without the encouragement I had as a child, I never would have found my way back to the theatre as an adult nor would I have written this book.

Finally, to all the children reading this book. Please keep dreaming as big as you possibly can. You are capable of more than you know, and anything can happen. Thank you for choosing my book.

Meet the Fossil sisters
in Noel Streatfeild's timeless classic,
Ballet Shoes